*B*LOOD:
THE NEW RED

*B*LOOD:
THE NEW RED

DAVID S. GRANT

OFFENSE MECHANISMS
PHILADELPHIA | NEW YORK

1

Always look like a rock star. This is the number one secret on how to be famous. I'm wearing chains, lots of chains. Eye shadow, lots of eye shadow. I wouldn't say my pants are tight, but then again, my balls might disagree with you at the moment.

I'm standing on the second level of the Grand Hotel, overlooking the bar area. My manager tells me this is where I need to be standing. In five minutes I will move across the room and stand next to a long mirror where one of the Hiltons will walk by and notice my reflection. A photographer will be close by and be sure to get the picture. This mirror has been placed here for this sole purpose. My manager tells me not to stare at the mirror. If you asked me to list my weaknesses, this may be my number one fault.

DJ Shingles, the newest (which means hottest) DJ, is playing on a middle level between the first and second floors. There is barely enough room for him let alone the overflowing ashtray and oversized stocking cap. Rumor has it this is his last show, despite this being his first. There is talk that he is moving into production and will be working with a major player in the hip hop industry, depending on who is hot at the time. DJ Shingles is wearing an Armani black button-down shirt with the sleeves ripped off. Very last year, but this is more a statement than a miscalculation on his part. Last season is the new season.

My manager signals for me to make my way across toward the mirror. A reporter from *GQ* is following me and asking me questions about who I'm going to sign with and whether or not my past will affect my future. I get her number, tell her I'll call her later, and then blow her off as I approach the mirror. Always leak your press, never tell. This is secret number three on how to be famous.

Four widescreen televisions are fastened to the wall behind the bar. All are showing TMZ. An orange haired girl wearing a Betsey Johnson dress sees me staring at the television sets. She walks over and whispers in my ear, "It's the new CNN."

A waiter carrying a tray of wine from 1980 is walking by. Every 15 minutes another waiter, another tray, another year will walk by. Welcome to the world of fashion parties. Ten percent content, ninety percent presentation.

A man who goes by the name Dontay hands me a coffee cup that is full of scotch. My manager tells me to sip it and not cheers anyone. Any buzz that insinuates I've been in rehab and have put my porn career in the past is good press and can only help my modeling career. As scheduled, I'm approached by someone with the last name Hilton.

The Hilton is wearing a blouse that is considered the color Ocean, the new blue, but since Aquamarine blue was in fact the new blue for last season and last season is in this season, no one should be caught dead in Ocean. Unless of course she is being ironic. If so, she will have to mention this to at least three people during the course of the evening.

"Mickey, you're back! I mean, uh..." Hilton looks at the coffee cup. "Welcome back!" She tips her coffee cup to me.

I glance around at the guest list, wondering who has the most juice at the party, but am distracted by the waiter walking through with wines from 1990.

"Good year for cabernets," Hilton says, then grabs her blouse. "Last season is the new season, huh? Fuck that." She laughs and looks fidgety as lights pop around us. At one point Hilton puts her arm around me and kisses me on the cheek. FLASH. Mission accomplished.

"I miss you, Mickey. We should get together sometime, you know, have a cup of coffee, fuck, or something."

Sure, I tell her and then she leaves because she has a rule about spending over forty hours a week on the Lower East Side and this season many Fashion Week parties have been in LES, the new SoHo.

According to my manager, I need to make my way to a reserved table next to the bar where Paul Johnson is sitting. My manager also says to ignore the temptation of champagne. I have a job to do tonight.

When I approach, Paul gets up from his table and gives me a hug. "Welcome back, Mick. We've missed you." I tell Paul great show and

3

congratulations on the new line, then look at the table and see they are all drinking 1986 chardonnay and there's a small mountain of cocaine in the center of the table. Paul looks at my cup and asks me if I need another coffee and I tell him I'm okay and then he proceeds to introduce me to the guests at his table, which include Lindsay Lohan, Jay Z, John Stamos, and four models I've never met but have bumped into during my previous job. One is a brunette with piercing blue eyes that I may have even shot a scene with but am not positive since I never saw much of her face. I pull out a pack of Camel non-filtered cigarettes and light one up. Paul asks me to join them. My manager agrees, so I grab a seat. The brunette tells me I look familiar, John Stamos says the same, and I grab a random razor from the ashtray and cut a line for myself.

Paul follows my lead, does a line and then lifts his head. There are still remnants of powder on his nose, but judging from his smile, he doesn't care. "Mickey, I want you to be my feature model, and I want to use you for my next project. What do you say?"

No one has ever turned down an offer from Paul Johnson, one of the top two designers in New York City. I consider saying no, just to make history, but my manager doesn't agree with this decision, so I put some cocaine on the razor blade and turn toward the brunette. On cue she lowers her dress, revealing her left nipple. I dump the coke onto the top of her left breast, move in, and snort it. She giggles and then says, "Now I remember you."

I excuse myself from the table because my manager has me scheduled to bump into Sandy Johnson near the men's restroom in three minutes. On my way to my spot, Dontay walks past and hands me a full coffee cup and slips me the number of John Stamos, "Just in case," he says.

Sandy exits the bathroom with his fly unzipped, hand in hand with Stan, his boy toy for the night, laughing and then flagging down a waiter holding a sign: 2002. My manager has strategically placed me between Sandy and the waiter so Sandy notices me and walks over. "Mickey! My God, you look fabulous!" Sandy gives me half-hug and cups my buttocks, then mentions that he has heard a lot of rumors involving me and the porn industry. I just laugh and tell him there's nothing wrong with franchising my body.

"Amen to that." Sandy turns to Stan and tells him to fetch him a glass of 2002 because he needs to talk business. Sandy surveys the scene and leans in to me. "Fabulous, isn't it?" I nod and then Sandy says, "Just murderous!"

Sandy moves next to me and puts his arm around my shoulder. "Did you see my show today?" It was great and congratulations I tell him but am cut off as he tries to say something, pauses, then finally says, "So I see you were talking with Paul."

I take a drink of Johnnie Walker and then say, "Yeah, actually he just offered me a job."

Sandy grabs his heart. "Oh, the betrayal! I think I'm going to faint." Stan appears out of nowhere with a chair for Sandy to sit down in and hands him a glass of wine. Sandy takes a drink and agrees that it is indeed 2002 and this seems to settle him. "Mickey, baby, we go way back. Your first runway, I believe. Honey, you need to come work for me, not that..." Sandy flickers over toward Paul, "beast!"

My manager tells me that I need to step outside because Juanita, my girl, can't get inside because she refuses to wear shoes and has just put out a joint on the bouncer's arm.

I tell Sandy thank you, and he says he'll be in touch. I lean into his ear and let him know his pants are unzipped and he says, "I know, it's the new sign."

I finish my cup of scotch and walk outside where Juanita is not only not wearing shoes but is also not wearing any pants, only a light purple Versace thong. The bouncer notices me and tells me that he doesn't have a problem with the thong, but there's a policy regarding the shoes. I let him know I understand and then buy a gram of cocaine off of him. I put Juanita in my limo and give her the gram to keep her busy. "I need to go inside and finish some business. I'll be right back," I tell her but she doesn't hear a word, already ripping open the gram and cutting three lines. "Thanks baby!" I hear her yell as I shut the door.

Back inside, my manager wants me to be on the right side of the bar because the glow from the light accentuates my features best. I look over and see Paul Johnson telling a story that I'm guessing involves a Hollywood movie star, too much champagne, and no panties while he decides which two models he is going to take home tonight. On the other side, Sandy Johnson is whispering into the ear of Stan and undoubtedly outing many of the stars here tonight. Presently, in between sips of three-hundred-dollar glasses of wine, they are pointing at Andy Garcia and nodding.

Paul Johnson versus Sandy Johnson, the two top designers in the city, fighting for the top spot. Fashion Designer of the Year. Earlier today Paul introduced a new line of furs despite the protest of PETA outside their tents at Bryant Park. At the end of the show Paul had all of his models come out onto the stage wearing nothing but fur and had a man with a wiry mustache throw goat blood all over all of them as Paul screamed, "It's the new red!"

Meanwhile, across the park, Sandy Johnson displayed his new men's line on the runway by having his male models hold the garments as they strutted naked and hard. Rumor has it there was no "fluffer" required. Sandy Johnson can be hands-on when required.

Both shows received standing ovations. The debate over which show was better continues. Paul versus Sandy, good versus evil, although in this case it is not clear who is playing which role. There was talk at one point that for Paul's next line, Eternal, a model would be executed on the runway.

As I light a Camel, my manager notifies me that Paul is approaching. "Mickey, be in my office first thing tomorrow." When Paul says tomorrow, he means 8AM tomorrow.

Too quick for even my manager to notice, Sandy comes up and asks me if I'm seeing anyone and I mention Juanita, which leads to a disappointed face and he tells me to stop by in the morning to discuss working for him. When Sandy says tomorrow morning, he means never.

My manager is noncommittal but pleased. We have accomplished our goal for the night. I glance over at Paul Johnson, then over at Sandy Johnson, the two kings, bitter rivals and not related. Simply known around the city as *The Johnsons*.

Walking out of the Grand, I look over at my limo. The window is rolled down and Juanita appears to have passed out. I walk over to my driver and tell him to take her home. As I turn back toward the club there is a TMZ camera in my face. "Mickey! Mickey! Who are you going with?" I light a Camel, remove my aviators, and look into the camera. "I'm going with Johnson! You can use that!" FLASH.

I reach into my pocket and grab the number of the *GQ* reporter and call her. We agree to meet at Lucky Sevens at Rivington and Stanton.

After we talk, she sends me a text message that reads: CAN'T WAIT TO GET MY LIPS AROUND YOU.

I go back to the doorway of the Grand (where I can hear "Mama Said Knock You Out" over the speakers), score another gram, stop off in the bathroom for a line, and then catch a cab to Lucky Sevens. In the cab the song "Suspicious Minds" by Elvis is playing. I cut a line and offer it up to the cab driver, who can't snort it fast enough. I do a line and sit back, smiling.

Act like you've lived this moment a hundred times over. This is the forty-third secret on how to be famous.

2

I'm lying on the bed in the Four Seasons. There are between two and three minutes where I lie shocked that I actually woke up after putting my body through last night's destruction. After hanging out with the *GQ* reporter, I ended up in an apartment above a cocaine bar in the West Village where obviously more coke was consumed. I'm not sure I've ever hit the plate as hard as I did last night.

Juanita is showering when I hear a knock at the door. A man who doesn't introduce himself hands me a medicine bottle with small illegible doctor-type scribbling on the side, and then quickly scurries off. There is a note attached on the bottle that reads:

Mickey:
Sorry I had to postpone our meeting this morning, but looking forward to seeing you this afternoon. Here is a gift, a small token, if you will, to help you get through the day.
You rock,
Paul

The bottle tells me that the pills are Vicodin. I pop one of them and it takes only five minutes before it hits me. I immediately dump out the bottle and count how many I have left. Eighteen.

One Christmas when I was young, I got a new Cannondale mountain bike, the kind with all the features, double brakes. Shit, it rode as smooth as a Cadillac. Until now, that was the most thoughtful gift I'd ever received, considering I would never go to the doctor to get a prescription. Can't stand the gowns—fashion disaster. My career would be over if someone got a shot of me in a gown.

Juanita is naked when she opens the door of the bathroom. "Was someone here?"

"No," I tell her and then I take another pill. Seventeen left. Cool.

She is drying off her thighs, exposing her bare breasts, then she looks up. "You look worn out, Mickey. I know you've only been back for a week, but maybe you should take a vacation."

I grunt, my head staring at the ceiling.

"Yeah, I've been hearing a lot about, oh now, what are those called?" She hangs up her towel and walks into the living room, next to the bed. "A man-cation. Yeah, that's it."

I lift my head. "No thanks. Remember, I was born in L.A., so I know what there is outside of New York. Mostly knuckle draggers."

Juanita opens a duffel bag and pulls out three bags of pot, all with labels on them that read: TRAIN WRECK, DRUNK DRIVER, and SUICIDE BOMBER.

"Don't smoke the SB," I tell her. "That's just not politically correct."

Juanita digs into her duffel and pulls out a wooden bowl that she packs with TRAIN WRECK and then she goes over to the flat screen and turns to a porn channel.

Looking at the television, I'm watching a threesome as Juanita comes over to the bed. Sensing I'm not able to move very well (but unknown to her it's because I'm numb from the double dose of Vicodin) she pulls off my robe and begins riding me, taking time-outs to hit off the bowl, until finally we finish and are forced to sit watching the porn channel even though neither of us is really into it at this point. I try to get up, but the Vicodin is making me unsteady. Luckily, Juanita finds the remote and turns the channel to Fuse, where we are forced to watch a Gwen Stefani video followed by The Fray. We are lying next to each other, both on our backs. Juanita is staring at our feet.

After a final hit off the bowl, Juanita asks, "What would be your trigger toe?"

Sensing my confusion, she continues, "Say you were going to, you know, off yourself with a shotgun. You place the barrel in your mouth but need to pull the trigger with a toe; your hands just don't reach." She shows me with her hands how this would be done.

I look down and tell her, "My big toe. My right big toe."

Juanita sighs. "No offense, baby, but your big toe is slightly angled. You'd hate to pull the trigger and be left with only a head wound. Not an easy job to finish off at that point."

"What about you?" I ask, looking down at her feet.

"My big toe is very straight and a little separated from the others, so mine is almost a perfect trigger toe."

Now I'm sitting up going back and forth between her feet and mine. "So what, are you saying my pinkie toe would be best?"

"Not sure, but it would be a much better choice than your big toe."

"I guess. Hey, do you want Thai food?"

Juanita nods so I order some food that we never get because we both nap for the next hour and don't hear the delivery person at the door.

Once awake I check my messages. Paul has confirmed a meeting for this afternoon, so I get dressed. The meeting is at four, but I have an appointment with a psychiatrist at three, so I need to get moving if I want to give myself some time to enjoy a little DRUNK DRIVER before I go. My manager tells me not to be late for my meeting with Paul.

Still naked, Juanita gives me a kiss and tells me good luck and then laughs because she knows I don't need it. The *GQ* girl calls and asks me what my plans are for tonight, and I let her know that I'm going to be out celebrating with some friends, but I may have a few minutes in between my appointment with Crazy Train and Paul Johnson.

"Crazy Train?" she asks.

"It's the new shrink phrase," I tell her, embarrassed she didn't know this already.

Inside the Crazy Train's office I'm wishing I'd never agreed to this. It was a French model, Nadine, who I wanted to meet who set me up only to convince me how good Dr. Shames really is. "Shames will make you think out of the box," Nadine assured me.

Assuming Dr. Shames was a woman, I'm disappointed when a man wearing a Macy's suit walks in and offers his hand. "Big fan," he tells me and then asks me to get out of his chair and move to the couch. I light a Camel and before he can say no I tell him this is not negotiable.

"You're used to getting what you want, Mickey, aren't you?"

I smirk. "You do know who I am then."

"Yes, I saw you on a billboard today."

"Cool." I take a drag off my Camel. "Which one? The one on Seventh or Spring Street?"

Dr. Shames asks about my porn career, which he refers to as my "previous venture." We discuss my childhood. Fun for me as a child was leaving L.A. and going to Tijuana for a day, where my friends and I could find trouble around any corner. Whether looking to score drugs, hookers, or just to get away from the California bullshit, Tijuana was our getaway, our form of camping. Many of the lessons in life I learned walking the streets. It's where I learned about women, losing my virginity at fourteen, and where I first experimented with drugs, several years prior.

14

After hearing this Dr. Shames looks annoyed and asks me more specific questions regarding fashion. "Do you feel pressure to be fashionable?"

I choke on my Camel. "Are you serious?" I stare at him. He is serious. "I *am* fashion. Whatever I wear is what is in. I could drape myself in blood and call it the new red and everyone would do the same."

Dr. Shames is scratching his chin. "So you feel you have a higher power when it comes to your job?"

I laugh, take a drag, and then blow smoke toward Dr. Shames. "Doc, I not only feel I have a higher power when it comes to fashion, look at me—I'm a fashion God." Like it or not, my manager reminds me of this each day.

I tell Dr. Shames I'm still having the card trick nightmares. Street performers surrounding me, doing card tricks. I try to look for a place to run away, but they are closing in. This is when I wake up in a cold sweat. Screaming.

Dr. Shames looks at his watch and signals that our time is up. "What about drugs?"

"What about them?" I ask back. "I'm over them. You know it was a popularity thing. It's not like you ever see only one person smoking a joint. It doesn't happen. It's in my past, or as you put it, left, along with my previous venture." The look in Dr. Shames eyes I've seen before, it's disappointment. He doesn't believe I've stopped using drugs.

Dr. Shames is my sixth shrink in the past twelve months.

My first therapist, Dr. Theodore James, was a believer in hypnotherapy. I have to say, I liked this and it helped me in a lot of ways. At a time when I was confused over the direction of my career, sessions of being under hypnosis provided clarity and also an outlet to reduce stress. Dude, Mickey can't be walking around with stress. That just is not cool. Dr. James had a tiger on his arm and let me call him Dr. J. He was very rock and roll and this is when I realized something had to go wrong. Always does.

Under hypnosis you are still in power, but in such a relaxed state the power of suggestion is much greater. After falling behind on condo payments, Dr. J. decided to begin making some extra cash by using his clients to rob banks, putting his patients under and then using their past to channel their energy toward bank heists. Of course, he could never use me because I might be recognized. Instead, he focused his criminal activity through regular, everyday people, women who would be inconspicuous. Who expects a middle-aged woman wearing mom jeans and a frayed sweatshirt?

After three successful jobs, the cops were onto him and his patients. After Dr. J., I was over with hypnotherapy. Dr. J. got ten years in federal prison, where I'm sure today he's out in the yard with other inmates telling them their eyelids are getting heavier...

After exiting Dr. Shames's office, I pop another Vicodin. Sixteen left.

3

Never admitting to a drug habit is the sixth secret on how to be famous. The exception is secret forty-seven: admitting to a drug habit only if it will enhance your career (i.e. the rehab stint).

Vicodin is running through my veins and DRUNK DRIVER continues to hang in my head when I walk into the corner office of Paul Johnson, located twenty-three floors up on Seventh Avenue. I look to the street on my left and I see Times Square and to my right the Empire State Building. Paul is smoking a cigar, blowing rings in the air, when I enter.

Paul stands but doesn't offer a hand since one is holding his cigar and the other is pointing.

I think back to an awards show where I saw Samuel L. Jackson and Morgan Freeman shake hands. That moment alone could have been a movie; the confidence along with the complexity was a thing of beauty. Once finished, they could have smoked a cigarette and no one would have said a word.

"Mick, welcome." Paul sits back down and stares at his computer. "What is it about people copying themselves on emails they send?" Paul hits the side of his computer monitor. "Anal retentive fucks!"

Next, Paul looks down at the New York Post; it is open to the movies section. "You know, before I got into this..." he makes a circle in the air with his pointing hand, "industry, I reviewed movies."

"Oh," is the only word that comes to my numb head.

"Yes, the only job I was ever fired at." Paul takes a puff from his cigar and blows more rings. We both wait for the circles to disintegrate, and then he continues. "There was a Nic Cage movie they wanted me to review, and I gave it a one-letter review—F." Paul laughs.

"What movie was it?" I reach into my pocket and grab a Camel.

Paul shuffles his feet. "That's exactly what my boss asked." He leans back. "I told him it doesn't matter, it's an overall review. F."

"Murderous," I say for some reason.

I chuckle, trying to think of Nic Cage movies and grading the ones I've seen in my head. I come up with a few C's like *Snake Eyes* and *Honeymoon in Vegas*, more D's like *Gone in 60 Seconds* and *It Could Happen to You*, and at least one F for *Leaving Las Vegas*.

"So I ended up here, but this wasn't my dream. I wanted to be a wrestling manager, you know, like the Hulk Hogan-type wrestling managers, but you know, that didn't work because I didn't like buses, so here I am. I guess you typically end up doing what you know," Paul smiles, "or in your case, what gift you are given."

A man wearing tight shorts and what appears to be an Italian made blouse interrupts our interview to ask Paul about a type of knit jersey fabric they need approval for. Paul stares at him for a second and then nods. The person wearing tight shorts leaves. Paul looks back at me.

"So anyway, happy April 20th. You know, 4-20? It's a little late, but I still like to say it. Myself, I enjoyed some fine Widow Maker straight from the Netherlands with my girls. Good stuff, just unfortunate that one of the girls, I think her name was Niki, kept insisting on rolling the joints. Women can't roll joints, but I'm not telling you anything you don't already know."

I nod. "No kidding. Most girls don't know shit."

Paul puts out his cigar. "I wouldn't go that far, I'm just saying rolling joints. Now, coke? Fuck it, line 'em up. Girls can cut rails. Pretty hard to fuck that up." Paul straightens himself up. There is a pause and then Paul says that last night he had a dream about putting an ex-girlfriend into a wood chipper. "I woke up with an erection." The word erection hangs in the air for a minute and then Paul realizes he's wandered off and leans in to talk to Mickey.

"So let me tell you why I need you, Mick. I'm not sure if you heard, but the city is creating a competition between me and Sandy, just the two of us. It's a fashion runway showdown, if you will, the quest to see who is the greatest—or biggest— Johnson in New York."

"You make great clothes," I say. I smoke my Camel while noticing the knife set displayed on the wall behind Paul. "What do you need me for?"

"A double team approach, if you will," Paul says.

I want Paul to clarify what double team means. Clarification on double teams is a personal rule I've used after the Sambo Brothers movie I did two years ago.

"Yes." Paul pulls out another cigar and puts it in his mouth but doesn't light it. "Let's take a walk. I want to show you something."

We leave Paul's office and head toward the Design area, having to first walk through the Finance and IT areas, where the phrase *there are so many women getting pregnant there must be something in the water* and associates explaining that *the jokes on cartoons are written for adults* is normal corporate discussion.

In the Design area, Paul grabs one of their latest production boards and shows me the new line, which consists of a lot of black with some red and everything fitting very tight. "What do you think?"

I'm about to tell Paul that it looks fantastic and fabulous and that he's a genius, but I'm cut off when Paul tells me, "It doesn't matter. It's about the show, the presentation. No one gives a shit about the clothes." Paul looks me in the eye. "They care about what the clothes mean."

"Okay, so this is why I'm here?"

"Sort of. I mean, you either have to have the model, like you, or you need to convince the consumer that there is a greater meaning to what you are selling."

"Like the quality?"

"No, not the fucking quality." Paul stares at me. I feel stupid. "Quality doesn't matter. Look at T-shirts today. Do you know how many T-shirt companies there are today? Thousands. Thousands of companies charging fifty bucks a T. Now does that have anything to do with quality?"

I don't answer. Instead, I reach inside for a Camel.

"Whatever fucking symbol they put on the T-shirts, the kids today, they think it's cool, or nostalgic. Shit, in Texas, one company sold out of all of their T-shirts that had a picture of a Q-tip on it. That's it, a fucking Q-tip. Do you know why?"

I shake my head.

"Because the kids adopted this as a way to tell who was into drugs. Fucking brilliant. That company made a billion dollars."

I smoke my Camel, high enough not to care about the relationship between the Q-tips, or how a billion dollars was made on them.

"I know what you're thinking—why Q-tips? Right?"

I shrug and take a drag.

"No one fucking knows. That's my point."

Okay.

A man wearing a graphic Tee (not a Q-tip) is talking loud about his date last night. "All I have to do is write the word BITCH on an envelope and drop it in the mailbox. It will get to him, oh yes, everyone knows." He is now waving his finger and slightly hopping.

Bruce, one of Paul's head designers, approaches with a pair of jeans that are not "working" because the factory messed up the measurements. "Sorry,

Paul, it looks like Production fucked up the samples. They all look like this. I feel like a total loser."

Paul grabs the jeans and grimaces. "Just fix the problem. Keep the fuckers up all night if you have to." He turns away and then turns back. "And you're not a loser because of this—you're a loser because you live in New Jersey. Move across the river. It will do wonders to your self esteem."

We continue our walk through Merchandising and Production, eventually ending up at his office. "I guess there are worse things than New Jersey. Take Alaska and Hawaii, for example. They don't even touch so I don't fucking count them as states. Fucking rebels is what they are."

I look at a small mirror next to the knife set and check my hair and cheekbones. Paul continues. "Oh well, you know what I always say? When life gives you lemons..."

I'm about to finish his sentence, but there is no time. Paul repeats, "When life gives you lemons, you should go buy a gun."

Paul finally lights his next cigar. "When you look around this place, you see a corporation I've built. Everyone knows their role, everyone does their job, and if they don't, I fire them on the spot. All have their checklists, dates, and goals. That's the problem. Other than myself, I don't have a face, if you will, and unfortunately, everyone knows me. I need someone new. I need you."

"Cool," I say and then reach for a Camel, almost accidentally grabbing my bottle of Vicodin. "I'm in, Paul. I'm ready to get back on the runway."

"I was hoping so. I know there was that whole European outsourcing movement the past couple years, but hiring an American model is the new European model."

More smoke rings. "This show, Mickey, you need to understand, is going to be over the top."

"Cool."

"No, you don't understand. You know how when there is a killer loose, or a hostage scenario, and the media is able to broadcast live? That event takes ownership of the news."

Paul laughs. "This is going to be the AMBER Alert of fashion shows. Mickey, we are going to own the news."

4

Four Designers stand as far back as possible from Sandy's new interviewee due to the stench. Sandy himself is making a permanent face with his nose crinkled as he asks questions to the man, who goes by Kung Fu Master on the streets.

Someone asks about Kung Fu Master's tax information and Sandy snarls something about not being able to claim alcohol despite being dependent.

He is a rare breed in New York City, a Japanese homeless person. Kung Fu Master is going to be the star of Sandy's showdown with Paul. One hour ago Kung Fu Master was begging for a dollar. If he got a dollar he was going to buy coffee, if he got more he was heading to the deli for beer. This was his only concern. FLASH. Someone snaps a picture of Kung Fu Master.

Wearing only a burlap bag and a fake gold chain attached to a plate that reads DIVA, Kung Fu Master is being told that he has just won the lottery and is going to make the front page of the very newspapers he has been using for blankets for the past four years.

5

For lunch I go to the Tuck & Go Seafood Restaurant, where Paul has me meeting a couple of his investors. James and Boyd are already at the restaurant drinking scotch. Back working in New York, each day I'm reminded of the way of life here. You are either an alcoholic on some level, or in AA. There is no in between, and many will be on one side or the other several times through their lifetime. Glasses half full, and James is already ordering a second round.

I have a light beer and listen to Boyd and James talk about the fashion industry and how they are big fans. I excuse myself to use the restroom and find quite the quandary. There are two restrooms, one for "Anchors" and one for "Life Savers". I stand for twenty minutes, staring back and forth, before going back to the table.

Next to us is a group of punks, all with tattooed sleeves and wearing leather jackets. It is eighty degrees outside, yet for this rare breed they will not break a sweat in these jackets. This is the type of shit that should be on the Discovery Channel. One of them is showing his latest tattoo, on his right arm. It is difficult to see since the whole arm is one long piece of work. For the tattoo artist, doing sleeves for the youth must be like winning the lottery. Each arm equals one mortgage payment.

I return to JOHNSON and go through a fitting of his new line, which, as he puts it, is still in the creative stage. I step out of Paul's office. Judy, a senior-level Design person I remember from a few years back (I may have slept with her, or at least she was in the room) enters his office. Judy is not even fully in the room before Paul is screaming at the top of his lungs, telling her the line is fucked, she has cost the company millions, and that she is not only fired but that he is going to sue her for the damage she has caused. I hear tears and then she screams.

I walk fast toward the elevator, remembering the industry from my first modeling days and how I despised these very people.

I sense my nerves getting the best of me, so I reach into my pocket. Fifteen left. I immediately feel better—no, indestructible is how I feel. The past comes back to me: the shows, the fans, the girls. Paul is right—it has nothing to do with the clothes; it's the presentation. That is why I own the industry.

A fine line between love and hate. Either way, you'll probably lose in the end, so enjoy the ride. The twenty-fourth secret on how to be famous.

Juanita and I meet on the corner of West Broadway and White and walk over to the loft on Franklin in Tribeca. We are greeted at the door by Star, Juanita's dealer—it's her party. She says, "Just call me Star, like Star Jones without the angry!" She cackles and then points to where the alcohol is in the kitchen. There doesn't appear to be any drugs, only alcohol. "That's interesting" says Juanita seeing the same thing.

Juanita takes off through the fast growing crowd and I decide to stay behind and head over to the kitchen to make myself a vodka rocks. Star comes over and I comment on the people and she says she has calculated the number of people will fill up the apartment enough that "You can feel the breath of your neighbor, but not their sweat!" She looks me in the eye then cackles, "Just kidding, we'll all be covered in sweat soon!" Then Star stands back and asks me why I am rubbing ice cubes on my chest and I don't have an answer. The reason is quite simple: I once knew a guy named Manny who used to rub ice on his chest before placing it into his cocktail. For some reason this has stuck with me and it feels good. Star is looking at me so I just stare at my chest and then back at Star who nods. Then there is an uncomfortable pause before she asks for one and puts it in her mouth. More cackling and then Juanita comes back, motioning across the room to a girl with orange hair who is dancing with some girls and then looks at me and says, "She's evil," and then I'm distracted because I'm picturing Juanita with the orange haired girl. The room is hot and we are both sweating. I make a vodka rocks for Juanita and freshen up my drink while we both look around at the people and that's when the theme begins to make more sense.

The guest list is very random. A passive guy with an Italian girl who is going around telling everyone her family is part of the Mafia—no, not the descendents, the actual fucking Mafia. The passive guy smiles and drinks a lot of vodka mixed with Sprite and leaves to go smoke every ten minutes. Outside on the terrace (where everyone is smoking) there is an Irish construction worker chain smoking Winston cigarettes. A gay man runs around inside letting everyone know that he is "in charge" of the syrup and yelling about needing a studded cod piece. There is a Spanish dancer who doesn't speak English. She is dancing with an Asian lesbian who came with two other Asian girls who are both drunk and talking to an annoying girl in a blue skirt who is unhappy with the last three movies she has watched. There is also a model with his girlfriend.

"This is going to blow up!" I say to Juanita, who looks back at me and smiles. "Sure is. Star is crazy." I wonder what Juanita bought from Star but am afraid to bring it up. Plus, I just dropped an ice cube down the front of my pants.

After only one hour there are at least sixty empty wine bottles, twenty empty liquor bottles, and the walls are covered in maple syrup. Thirty minutes later, neighbors are banging on the door, three people are getting trampled because they passed out, and syrup is dripping from the ceiling. Star stands on her small coffee table and announces, "The birth of chaos!"

This leads to more liquor, more wine, and then Juanita begins kissing the Spanish dancer. The Spanish dancer comes over, wipes syrup from her lips and puts her fingers in my mouth. "I know who you are. You're Mickey!" She grins.

Juanita comes over and she is covered in syrup and carrying a bottle of tequila. We both take a couple pulls and then Star lets everyone know it's time to leave by playing Jefferson Starship's "We Built This City."

6

Paul Johnson wakes up each morning to a playlist that contains Bon Jovi's "You Give Love a Bad Name", Billy Joel's "Captain Jack", "No More Mr. Nice Guy" by Alice Cooper, "Beautiful People" by Marilyn Manson, and several other songs by Justin Timberlake given to him by his Design team for this season's inspiration.

Each morning his maid from Brazil (wearing only a black thong) serves Paul two waffles with a healthy dose of syrup spread over the top along with a side plate of bacon. A glass of champagne, which is usually half-gone once he finishes his meal, is Paul's beverage of choice. He finishes the rest of his drink while being orally pleasured by his maid. This has been his morning routine for the past ten years.

After she's finished (now timed perfectly to Paul's last sip of champagne), Paul turns on his phone, which already contains twenty voicemails. Despite Paul's birthday occurring a month ago, the industry has decided that tonight it will be celebrated. Rumor has it that over half the Playboy Bunnies will be there, including two of Hugh Hefner's current girlfriends. Paul has a message from a man named Chunky on the rules of the Bunnies. "Pretty much there are no rules, unless it's one of Hef's girls. Then it's best to just stay away." Paul listens to the rest of his calls in his town car as he is driven from the Upper West Side down to Seventh Avenue.

You could say Paul Johnson was a child of the Garment Industry. His father, Robert Johnson, built a company from the ground up called simply JOHNSON, then once Paul worked his way up changed it to JOHNSON & SON, and then when sales dropped back to JOHNSON. After working his way up to the VP level, it was Paul who left and consulted around the world, focusing on the cutting edge couture fashion as well as the over the top marketing of products worldwide. It was during a night in Tokyo after a lot of sake when Paul realized that the garment produced wasn't nearly as important as the presentation. When Paul returned to the family business, his father became ill and Paul took over the line, shortly turning JOHNSON from a boutique-type company to a major player in worldwide retail. Paul Johnson's outrageous business plans, shocking lines, and over the top fashion shows were legendary after only a few years. No one came close until a new line called simply "J" was presented by a designer named Sandy Johnson.

In his office, Paul's phone continues to ring, mostly calls regarding the birthday party. What tapas would he prefer? Any lighting requests? Does it matter which outfits the Playboy Bunnies wear? Dennis, one of Paul's designers, enters his office to show him a new sketch for a woman's blouse with pockets.

"I can't take full credit for the side," Dennis points to the drawing, "I totally stole this from two seasons ago."

Paul pulls out a cigar and lights it. Dennis looks at the smoke permeating from his stogie and tells Paul, "You know, now listen to this, this is really fabulous. You know how cigar is spelled with a C? Well think about it—so are the words Competent, Calm, and Confident." Dennis smiles, almost drooling. "Doesn't that exemplify what a cigar smoker is, how they come across?" Dennis actually jumps a little bit off the ground. Paul is staring at him. "And don't forget Clinton, he was a C, and he's got a great cigar story, and of course... Oh wait, I'm just rambling like a crazy man, and oh my God, I have to get over to Barney's in like five minutes. See you, Paul." Dennis leaves.

Paul smokes his cigar and stares at his office entrance for the next five minutes.

In the early afternoon Paul walks over to the conference room where his Production team is reviewing the calendar for the next product line. It's more tricky than usual because not only is there the regular business but also the exhibition is coming up, so resource planning is the main topic.

Paul calls everyone around for a pep talk. It takes a few minutes for everyone to break away from their draping and phone calls, finally gravitating toward the center of the room.

"Listen, everyone. I know I'm harping on the same shit, but this needs to be the best we can do. Fucking nirvana. That's what we're looking for."

Paul takes a deep breath, noticing that some of his team looks preoccupied.

"Look at it this way, during the French Revolution, when the guillotine was in full effect, it would chop off a person's head." Around the circle there is a collective look of horror and peering over shoulders hoping for a Human Resources representative to join them.

"When a head was chopped off, it would still have eight to fifteen seconds when the brain still worked. That eight to fifteen seconds is what I want this line to be."

It takes the team much longer to get back to work than it did for them to break away.

As Paul sees it, the work itself, from the Production side, is pretty straightforward: Inspire. Create. Repeat.

His job is to motivate.

Around 8pm, guests begin arriving at Paul's party, located at The Cellar, where the Playmates feel very much at home. Anna, who was Miss March, is hanging on Paul as he talks to Jamie Foxx about the latest Ferrari and how the previous model handled better. They both agree that the leather in the newer model sweats too much. After taking a second to think about this, both nod approvingly.

7

I arrive sometime around 9pm and can barely see because there are so many people. I've already had three bottles of wine, a half bottle of tequila, and the cigar smoke is hanging like fog. I overhear some hayseed at the bar saying that they have everything: whiskey, coke, and Sun Chips.

Luckily, Paul spots me and yells, "Hey Mick!" and then I notice the Playmates and I know I'm in the right spot. Paul offers me a cigar dipped in scotch and then introduces me to Jamie Foxx, who recognizes me from one of my adult films, and then I spot two girls who look familiar so I leave and am relieved when I realize that I don't know them and that they are Playmates.

We find ourselves in a private room, drinking champagne and smoking a joint. Both girls tell me I'm the most beautiful person they've ever seen and that this was a good move by Paul. I offer them a Vicodin and am pleased when they don't accept, then, with my aviators on, I have sex with both of them (at one point Kate Moss popped her head into the room, but we all ignored her), and then as I'm putting on my pants they both giggle and say we should keep this a secret so their boyfriend doesn't find out, and that's when I realize I've just fucked two of Hef's girls.

8

Around 10pm, Paul is notified that Sandy Johnson will not be attending. Paul shrugs his shoulders and yells an insult that no one can actually make out but all fully understand. At 10:30pm there is an announcement that the octopus appetizer is tainted and it is advised that anyone who had it go to the hospital immediately. Since no one in the industry eats, this announcement only sends a couple corporate associates to the doors. At 11pm "Happy Birthday" is sung to Paul, who leads all in a toast predicting victory over Sandy and to once again bring JOHNSON back to number one. Inspire. Create. Repeat.

At midnight, Paul notices the Playmates heading to the door, causing all to follow, so he inquires as to why and this is when he receives the news that there has been an incident. The man, a PR officer from Playboy, is talking to Paul while motioning over to me.

Paul calls over me, we talk briefly, and then Paul says, "Oh well, have to expect this with you. You're Mickey. Look at you, you're like a god."

When someone refers to you as a god, always give a reassuring nod. This is the ninth rule of how to be famous.

The after-party is lame. Not due to the attendees, but rather the location of Times Square.

I hang out with a new band from Brooklyn named NITRIS for a while, drinking Bass and smoking Camels. The lead singer, who goes by Nail, offers me a brownie that I eat and it immediately has a reaction with the other drugs in my body. When the band members hear what I've consumed prior to the brownie, their only response is, "Hang on, man. You need to ride it out."

The guitarist of the band, who goes by Predator, gives me his iPod and tells me to play the playlist titled "Kicked in the Balls". I go to the corner and fall to the floor. I find the playlist and am relieved it's jazz and light blues music because no other music can bring you down quite the same way. I nod to the trifecta of Coltrane, Armstrong, and Vicodin and then nod off.

Four hours later, I wake up. The iPod is gone and I'm the only person left in the party room. I let myself out the back, rats scurry as I open the door, and I go back to the hotel.

9

At JOHNSON headquarters, on Seventh Avenue, Paul is having a meeting with his executive team. Paul has acquired the best of the best regardless of their specialty. The philosophy being that if you are good, you are Johnson material. Each has his differences with Paul and each has considered leaving; however, so far Paul has rewarded their loyalty and JOHNSON is one of the top two, so no one has yet to make that next move.

To the left is Amal, the CIO and ex-techie nerd who, despite having difficulty understanding the lingo, has streamlined JOHNSON to one of the shortest production calendars in the industry. Josh, the CFO, sits next to Amal with his glasses perched on the tip of his nose. Josh's job is to ensure not a penny more than necessary is spent. This is not only his job, nor only his heritage (long line of Jewish tax attorneys), but is his passion as well. Stan, the portly COO, is the other person at the table. At the moment he is eating a large plate of ham and eggs. There is a fifty percent chance that Stan will point with his fork during the meeting.

"I have to be victorious, and will need my generals focused!" Paul slams down his hand. "Nothing is more important than this exhibition! We have less than a month to design and present this new line, and if we don't deliver, we lose, and then as far as I'm concerned, you will all be fired. All gone. I'll hire a new team. Shit, I don't know how all of you have been around so long." Paul looks down at his watch. "If you remember one thing, remember that Sandy Johnson is my sworn enemy and I will do anything to fuck him." Paul pauses, "Because god knows he'd do anything to fuck me!" There is laughter throughout the room. "Fuck, I have to meet with the Design team now and present my vision for the exhibition. Does anyone have any questions?"

No one says a word, each nodding and looking at each other around the table. Paul walks out.

10

"Socially Impotent" is the phrase Sandy uses to describe society and its taste in clothing.

Two buildings down from JOHNSON, Sandy is rallying his team, which is a bit distracted because Benny, Sandy's head Designer, has just arrived wearing tight camouflage clothing and has confessed that he finally spent the night with the Merchandiser from Barney's and that they are already planning to go to the Cape over the weekend. It's obvious that Louie, from Accessories, is jealous (he also had a crush on the Barney's boy) because he storms away from the group and it's up to Sarah from Technical Design to run after him and talk him down and back into the group. Once everyone is back together, Sandy continues, "Socially Impotent...

"Now listen, ladies, and listen closely. This is my—our—chance to make it. If I beat that man-beast Paul, we are all winners. Let's fucking rock everyone's world."

The homeless man, Kung Fu Master, enters the area. Sandy introduces him and then informs everyone that the line to be designed is inspired by the combination of Nineties Paris and Eighties Duran Duran, and the line formerly called "Bent" is now going to be called "Just Do Me." Sandy ends his speech with "Now get to work and create something that makes you want to get laid!"

Everyone applauds except for Kung Fu Master, who is eating a sandwich and drinking from a bottle of Chianti. He nods approvingly.

11

Back at JOHNSON, Paul is in front of the full Creative and Production teams. Paul points to a boy wearing a shirt that reads FASHION POLICE and he walks over to a stereo and pushes a button. Boston's "More Than a Feeling" is blasting through the design studio speakers.

"We need to tear down the past and build something new." Paul looks around the room, making eye contact with each person regardless of their Assistant or Vice President titles.

"Team, you have to destroy present ideas to truly create something new. Inspire me with your idea, create your wildest thoughts, and then—and only then—will you be able to iron out the details."

Paul paces in front of the room and repeats the word "Destroy" over and over for two minutes and then says, "Create."

Inspire. Create. Repeat.

CFO Josh approaches from behind with a large board covered with a light blue cloth. On cue, Josh steps away and Paul turns around, grabs the cloth, and rips it away, unveiling the name of the new line. Jaws drop and random gasps are heard. Josh nods approvingly. The board reads: A LINE OF SELF DESTRUCTION.

Paul points again to the boy in the FASHION POLICE shirt who again pushes a button. This time it's Journey, "Don't Stop Believin'". As soon as the song starts everybody gets up and begins dancing. Paul lights up a cigar and looks around the room, nodding approvingly.

12

As Paul is informing his company of the new line and how it will be represented, he already has me traveling around the country promoting his new LINE OF SELF DESTRUCTION, to be debuted at the Johnsons' Runway event. First, I arrive at O'Hare, where I do a fashion shoot at the Hilton for an hour (the photographer got into the business ten years ago based on one pose I did for a French designer), then I hop back on a plane and head to South Beach, where I'm pressed between two men in Speedos who won a contest to meet me and have their picture taken (both hit on me constantly until finally I agreed to come back for a weekend), and then finally it's off to L.A., where I have two interviews (one with a Hollywood Insider show and the other with some columnist who wants to be the insider in the fashion world but clearly doesn't have the lips for it), a dinner with the editor of the new fashion magazine SWING (he hits on me consistently until I agree to meet him in South Beach), and three other magazine shoots either wearing various JOHNSON items or having them close by as my greased body is photographed thousands of times. My last shoot is with Pedro Morales from Amigos magazine. He had me wear a sombrero, which leads me to begin telling tales of nights where I have either received or ended the night wearing a sombrero. Once finished, a concerned Pedro approaches me in private and tells me that three or more sombrero stories may mean I have a problem. He pats me on the back and says, "Food for thought, amigo!"

Finally, around midnight I get to my hotel, where I have a message from Tonya, an old friend I did a movie with, asking me if I want to go to a "P cubed" party, where it's like a potluck party but with pills. Each brings their own bottle. Pill Potluck Party. I open up my bottle of Vicodins and realize there is no way I could ever give one of them up. I pop one of the pills, jerk off to one of my old movies, and fall asleep. Thankfully my manager has arranged for a pickup the next morning to get me in a car and take me to the airport because the next thing I remember is getting into a limo at LaGuardia.

My manager tells me I did well but need to lay off the drugs. With the constant industry buzz, I am headed back to number one, and I don't need to ruin my second chance. You only get one comeback. Then my driver hands me a bag of the finest cut cocaine I've ever seen in my life.

13

Sandy Johnson wakes up each morning around 11am to a playlist containing Elton John's "Rocket Man", The Beach Boys' "Surf Girl", Tina Turner's "Private Dancer", and Timbaland's complete catalog of music.

Raul, Sandy's Spanish butler, has his grapefruit juice (with a shot of vodka) waiting for Sandy as he approaches the dining room. After sipping his juice, two egg-whites, a half-slice of bacon, mango, and oral sex from Raul follows.

"Good luck," are two words of Raul's limited vocabulary that he says to Sandy on his way out, not looking back but instead focused on the tapas selection to be served this evening at a party he's throwing to celebrate his new headshots to be used to promote the design exhibition against Paul Johnson. Vicki, one of Sandy's assistants, calls and asks if Sandy would like any Playmates at the party, "You know, Paul had Playmates at his birthday party," Vicki tells Sandy.

"Playmates? Girl, what the fuck am I going to do with Playmates? You're high as a kite crazy is what you are. No, wait—see if any Chippendales are available."

Minutes later, Sandy is sitting in the office of Dr. Colleen McDowell, his psychiatrist, who is asking Sandy about the past couple days, also his upcoming event.

"How do you feel about Paul Johnson? There seems to be a bit of animosity between the two of you," McDowell asks.

Sandy crosses his legs tightly, lightly kicking his right foot, showing the emblem of his K-Swiss sneakers. "He's arrogant and selfish and his style, oh God, it makes me so angry!" Sandy stands up and begins pacing. "What was the question?"

"How do you feel about Paul Johnson? Judging from the papers, the two of you are trading some rather personal barbs."

"Beast. I fucking hate him." Sandy stops for a moment and turns. "And by the way, is he paying you?" Sandy waits for McDowell's response, but she refuses to play along. "No, he's not paying you, so let's stop fucking talking about him and focus on the more important of the two Johnsons." Sandy's arms flail as he says this and then he pulls out some pictures of his new headshots and hands them over. "Aren't they fantastic? I hope they're not too shocking. I want fabulous, but not shocking. What do you think?"

McDowell views them and approvingly nods. Sandy continues, "I'm having a party tonight at 45th and Park if you want—"

"I can't," McDowell says quickly. "I mean, I have plans, and also it may not be that good of an idea."

Sandy sits back down. "Whatever, just offering you fun. It's not like I was asking you out for a date." Both laugh. "Oh well, let me know if you change your mind, or if you ever need to just blow off steam." Sandy looks down at McDowell's legs.

"Believe it or not, I even know a few straight men who could remove all of your stress."

"I'll keep that in mind. Sandy, how are the headaches? Are they still happening?"

"Still there. I think it's that I just don't like people, which is weird because I need to be around people, so maybe that's not it."

"Maybe it's that you need their acceptance."

"Okay, Miss Doctor, are you insinuating that I'm just another whore in the fashion industry who does whatever it takes, bends over for anyone who asks, all for acceptance?"

McDowell sits up. "No, I meant—"

"Yeah, I know, I was just being hot shit. Hey, do you have any cocktails here?"

"Okay, let's go a different direction with this." McDowell adjusts her seat, moving him higher in her chair. "What about the dreams? Are you still having the dreams?"

Sandy moves his head side to side. "Sort of, well, not as often."

"Still the same, though?"

"Yes, I'm on the phone with my dream man—you know, about twenty-one, Italian, with Abercrombie abs."

"Yes." McDowell smiles, then pushes Sandy along.

"And, well, he invites me over to his place, so of course I go over there, but no one answers the door. Finally I turn the knob and open the door, walk in and yell for my man, but instead of seeing him, out comes Chris Hansen from Dateline."

Sandy takes a deep breath. "I still don't understand." A pause and then Sandy asks, "What do these dreams mean?"

"It's not good, Sandy. The dreams, though, they've cut down, not as often?" asks McDowell.

"Oh, yes. Now it's only once a night." Sandy pauses. "You really need to serve cocktails in here."

14

Known simply as "Ralph the Tipper" for his legendary thousand-dollar tips, Ralph is much more than just a healthy tipper, and seeing him talking to Sandy at his HEADSHOTS party is creating quite a stir.

Ralph is a consultant in the industry during fashion weeks, where it is his job to create drama. Two years ago, when he was hired by Paul Johnson, Ralph was the brains behind the whole throwing fake blood on the models (a preemptive strike against the PETA people, followed up after the show by throwing fake blood on them). To this day there is gossip that only a percentage was fake and that the rest of the blood was from the animals used to create the furs during the show.

Fear and nervousness is felt through the party, particularly by the models who will be used for the upcoming exhibition. Of course, Kung Fu Master doesn't seem distracted as he is at the bar having mixed shots of José Cuervo and Grey Goose in his honor. These shots are complimentary and are called the Kung Fu Mother Fuckers for one night only.

After talking with Sandy, Ralph walks over to the bar and orders a dirty martini, extra olives. Ralph winks at a waitress and motions for her to approach. She comes over and Ralph hands her the martini, she walks away, and then Ralph orders another one. When the bartender hands it to him, Ralph drops a hundred on the bar, takes a sip, and then leaves.

15

The next day, back in Dr. McDowell's office, the topic is Sandy and his years growing up known to him as "The Zima Years."

"Like I said before, it was tough for me because I was told early on that guys only hang out together if they are partying or gay, and I didn't do drugs when I was young." Sandy looks up at the ceiling and then back to Dr. McDowell. "I didn't have Entourage, I had Growing Pains."

McDowell crosses her legs. "So you think that's why you're gay?"

Sandy laughs. "Oh God no. It's just strange, don't you think?" Sandy crosses his legs.

"I'm gay because I'm a Taurus. I totally believe our sexuality and personalities are totally derived from horoscopes and the tide."

They discuss whether Sandy was sexually active during these years, which leads to Sandy requesting a calculator and a cocktail. After an attempt to calculate sexual numbers, he no longer wants to discuss "The Zima Years" anymore. Sandy changes the conversation to competition. Sandy challenges McDowell to see how far she would go to be the best.

McDowell, confused, scrunches her face. "I'm not sure I understand the question."

Sandy smiles. "Let me put it this way, if you could guarantee victory against your arch nemesis, how far would you cross the line?"

Sandy is out the door before McDowell can say another word.

16

Paul is looking out the window, onto 56th Street, wondering since he was out of the office whether any work was being done back in the office.

Dr. Melissa Zimzuber sits across from him in her leather chair while Paul moves away from the window, over to the couch, pulling out a cigar and lighting it.

"So again, Paul, we've covered the—as you call them—'The Busch Light Years', and other than that, you pretty much have it all, yet you feel lonely and unsatisfied." Dr. Zimzuber walks over to the window and cracks it, allowing the cigar smoke to escape. "I've got to say, a lot of people would like to be you."

Paul blows a smoke ring into the air and frowns, then looks over at his doctor. "You know, had we not fucked right here on that very table," Paul points to the desk, "I would fucking leave after a question like that."

Paul stands up, then sits back down. "Who the fuck wants to be like me? They don't know me." Paul's cell phone rings. He grabs it, tells someone to fuck off, and then continues, "And another thing—I never said I was lonely. Not satisfied, yes, but not fucking lonely. Do you see me eating alone, eating TV dinners while listening to Eleanor Rigby, or any of that shit?"

Paul doesn't give her a chance to respond.

Paul blows smoke at the doctor. "No, you fucking don't."

Paul leaves.

17

A rare night not traveling, and in the city, Juanita and I meet up with one of my old friends, who goes by the name of Stardust, at a rooftop bar in Murray Hill named FUSED. Stardust and I worked together when we were both fifteen (or at least we told the agencies we were fifteen). We did mostly foreign magazines, some runway work.

Stardust is talking about his first time and how he had "gotten to third base a number of times but never made it home."

"Yeah, but blowjobs are pretty close to home," I tell Stardust.

Our waiter comes over. Juanita orders gin on the rocks, Stardust has some type of scotch I've never heard of, and I order a vodka tonic.

Stardust is making a special request with his drink, then he turns back. "But dude, I didn't get a blowjob. That's not third."

"Sure it is. The four F's: French, feel, fellatio, and fuck."

Stardust almost jumps out of his seat. "Those aren't the four F's. It's French, feel, finger, and then fuck."

I look over at Juanita, then back to Stardust. "You sure?"

"Dude, of course." You can see something crossing Stardust's mind. "Wait, your F's sound like you gave a blowjob, dude. That's fucked up."

"No man, it's a receiving thing," I tell Stardust as our drinks arrive. "Anyway, are you telling me you never got a blowjob until after you had sex?"

Stardust slams his full drink and calls the waitress over and orders another one, first asking if Juanita and I are okay. Neither of us has tasted our drink yet. Stardust turns back. "Yeah, I guess that's true. The girls where I grew up just didn't do that."

"Wow, that's strange," I say. "There's, like, no reason to give them coke then."

"What?" Stardust is looking for his next drink.

I finally take a drink of mine, then decide to slam it as the waitress brings over Stardust's second one. I order another then say, "You know, I guess we really grew up in different places."

After four more drinks, Stardust is walking sideways. Juanita has only had two, but she is tired so she goes home, while Stardust and I decide it's a good idea to have a couple more drinks. We go to an Irish pub named McKinley's and both do shots of whiskey followed by another round of shots that the bartender refers to as "not quite gasoline."

After McKinley's, we walk into a bar named THE GO-GO ROOM, thinking there would be dancing, but instead we get a surprise. As soon as we enter, the bartender locks eyes on Stardust and jumps over the bar, coming at him hard. The bartender grabs Stardust and throws him down. The bouncer comes over, grabs Stardust off the floor, and holds him so the bartender can take a clean swing at him. I lunge at the bartender, but before I can get my arms around him, two guys from the bar grab me and hold me back. Stardust takes four shots to the face (two roundhouses and two uppercuts) and numerous body shots before he falls to the ground. Stardust is spitting up blood while grabbing near the side of his jeans, where he pulls out a butterfly knife and makes a backward stabbing motion, catching the bouncer in the knee. The bouncer goes down and Stardust swipes at the bartender, nicking his arm, just enough to draw blood. The two guys from the bar let go of me and I grab Stardust and we run. Two blocks later we stop, looking back, catching our breath.

Breathing heavy, I can barely get out, "What the fuck was that about?"

"I think I had sex with the bartender's wife."

Still hunched over, Stardust asks me for a Camel, after which he says, "She gave me a blowjob, too."

18

I take the first flight out of JFK, going back to Chicago, where Paul is going to be a guest on Oprah today. On the plane a girl with green hair asks me if I want to see her pussy. Before I am able to answer she pulls up her pant leg and exposes a tattoo of a cat on the back of her leg. She asks if I would like to pet it. I put my seat back, put on my aviators, and try to ignore the crazy cat woman the rest of the flight.

My manager has arranged for a girl named Sage to meet me at the airport and ride with me in a limo downtown. Sage is waiting outside of the limo, wearing only a purple camisole, four-inch heels, and a tight black skirt. Our first stop is a private gym, where I run for thirty minutes on the treadmill, climb for twenty minutes on a Stairmaster, followed by three sets of squats and a thousand crunches. After I shower and return to the limo, I find Sage (who has been waiting there) seductively lying down in the limo holding a glass of champagne, and now only wearing her camisole, her skirt discarded on the floor of the limousine next to an empty bottle of Cristal. She moves next to me and gives me a handjob while I listen to my messages. The first is from Paul, letting me know he'll meet me in the green room. My manager tells me that the limo should be arriving at the studio in ten minutes and that I should meet Paul in the green room. I listen to another message, this one from Juanita, telling me to "break a leg, babe" for whatever it is I'm going to do for Paul. I listen to the new song by The Dirty Pearls, drink down a glass of champagne, and smoke a Camel.

Once we arrive at the studio, Sage hands me a package with the shirt I'm going to be wearing and tells me the limo will be waiting to take me back to the airport once the show is finished. I ask her what she is going to be doing and she opens a side compartment to reveal another full bottle of Cristal and a vibrator that is shaped like a miniature leopard and has a silver racing stripe on its back. As I step out, she hands me another package. "This is for you." I can tell it's from my manager. It's my bottle of Vicodin.

Inside the green room, Paul is surrounded by show interns and a woman who is clearly a hooker but is being called Paul's assistant for the next hour. Paul is smoking a cigar when one of the interns offers him a Red Bull, which he shoots down. "You kidding me? I can't have one of those! I have one of those, in thirty minutes I'll be running the halls looking for coke."

Knowing when not to mix uppers is the fifty-first secret on how to be famous.

"How about something light, a soda or beer?"

Paul orders a beer.

"Would you like a glass?"

Paul looks at the intern, astonished. "Of course! What are we, truckers?"

Paul looks over at me and then over at his date. I nod approvingly. He moves closer. "These girls in the north, not exactly grade A, know what I mean?" Paul jabs my ribs with his elbow.

"The smart ones, they all head south. Nothing like warm weather to put you in better spirits." Another jab to my rib. "Especially when you're working the corner."

I light a Camel and am staring at the mirror when Oprah comes back for a second and introduces herself to me and then gives Paul a heartfelt hug and they exchange pleasantries. Oprah gave Paul a huge break years back, allowing his line to be shown on her show, but since throwing blood on his models during one of his shows, he has gotten the cold shoulder, until now, where it appears to be "blood under the bridge," as Paul jokes.

The show starts and Paul is introduced and he goes out to the stage, sitting next to Oprah. In the green room, his assistant walks up to me and presses her ass against my right thigh and asks, "Is there ANYTHING I can do for you?"

I quickly say no and feel a chill down my spine when I think about what kind of shape Sage will be in once the show is done. I may take a taxi back to the airport.

Paul has the audience in stitches when he lets them know they are all going to get a blazer from his new collection. When Paul describes the new line, he uses the phrases "a line of self destruction" and "a line of love".

Oprah asks specifically what he means and Paul follows with, "Well, it's very natural. First, to achieve true greatness in anything, you have to erase—or forget, if you will—the past and start over. You have to destroy the past."

"And you feel this is natural?" Oprah asks.

"Of course. How else can you go places no one else has gone before?" Paul takes out a cigar (unlit) and places it in his mouth.

Oprah continues carefully, "Okay, how do destruction and love fit together?"

Paul laughs. "Because true love is self-destruction." Paul looks out at the audience, many sitting at the edge of their seats. "Now I'm not sure if you," Paul points to the audience, "or anyone else have experienced love like me." Paul takes the unlit cigar and moves it from his left hand to his right hand. "True love, mad love, is that moment during passion—not sex, mind you—but that moment of passion where you take a knife, give it to your significant other, rip open your shirt, and tell her to go for it, just stab me right in the heart!" Oprah gasps, but before she can show her disgust, the crowd gets on their feet and applauds. After a break, Paul introduces me as the one and only male supermodel whom he trusts to show his new line. I come out wearing a polo tank shirt and oversized aviators, strutting across the stage, stopping near Oprah's chair, where she feels the collar and brushes up against my abs.

Paul can sense that Oprah is both impressed and uneasy so he pushes it, asking her to be a part of his runway show during the exhibition. The audience returns to their feet. Paul assures Oprah that there won't be any blood and that he is not only past that phase but that he has learned from the experience. After this admission, the crowd cheers ever louder and Oprah is forced to agree to be part of his show. As she accepts, her management team is already working on a way to get her out of it.

After the show, in the green room I'm watching Paul making calls, getting his people in line to work with Oprah and ensure she is part of his show. It's at this time I remember what Paul told me: "We are going to take over the news."

On my ride back to the airport, Sage is completely naked and somehow still conscious. At first she jumps up on me, putting her crotch in my face, but then she falls backward onto the floor of the limo. She cracks her head on an empty champagne bottle, removes my shoe, and starts playing with my little toe, rubbing and then placing it in her mouth. I jerk my foot back, but she gets angry and grabs my foot again, moving on from the little toe to the larger ones until she gets to the big toe. She caresses it for ten minutes and then sucks on it for another five. After she fills a garbage bin with champagne and dips my foot inside. She pulls out my foot and puts it into her mouth. She fits my whole right foot into her mouth, my big toe sliding down her throat.

Always give a naked girl what she wants is the twenty-ninth secret on how to be famous.

Five more minutes and we arrive at the airport. Sage lights a cigarette and with little effort does a wave as I put on my socks and shoes and then leave. I feel dirty and used when I arrive inside the terminal.

I call Juanita and she asks, "How did it go?"

I tell her I think my foot was just raped and she laughs and says that she can't watch daytime talk shows either.

19

FLASH. Bulbs pop to my left and right as Juanita and I walk the red carpet of the annual New York City Design Awards. Both of the Johnsons are being recognized for their years of achievements, naturally creating even more of a buzz for the exhibition. A woman from E! named Tamara wants to interview me, but the two Vicodins I took earlier have made my mouth dry so I kiss her on the cheek and tell her she should just call me because hearing about how great my life is will not make her feel better about hers. I light a Camel and let her take pictures of me at her side.

As we walk in, Juanita asks if I'm nervous about introducing Paul and I just laugh because she obviously doesn't know just how fucked up I am. "Sure are a lot of beautiful people here," says Juanita.

"Sure are, babe." I pull her closely as the New York Post takes our picture for page six. "Beauty here is natural. It's like fires in Detroit, babe."

Backstage I'm adjusting the tie on my Armani tuxedo when Paul grabs my shoulder to steady himself. Clearly he has been to a few of the pre-parties and has gotten himself lit up. "Remember when you introduce me not to say too much. We want all of it to be a surprise." Paul sees a waiter pass, calls him over, and orders a scotch. "We—me and you, Mickey—we're going to take over the whole fucking place."

I really don't know what Paul is talking about.

Not knowing where he is going and definitely not in a steady state to comprehend, I put my hand on his shoulder and tell him not to worry about anything.

Paul lights a cigar as his scotch arrives and says, "Doesn't matter. Once you're in front of the microphone, you're a liar. Anyone who wears a black turtleneck, or has a microphone in front of them," Paul takes a drag off his cigar, blowing the smoke straight up, "there's a ninety-percent chance they're either lying to you or they're a serial killer."

Paul goes to scratch himself and accidentally drops his cigar. "Fucking whore!" Paul yells, drawing looks from several people standing close by, including Katie Couric, who looks especially appalled.

Paul grabs another cigar. "Last night I tried a new service that was recommended to me. So she shows up looking like an in-house call girl. What the fuck?"

He lights his cigar. "So she shows up, twenty minutes late, mind you, and has the nerve to ask me for all of the money up front. Again, what the fuck?" Paul takes a long drag off his cigar, blowing the smoke out slowly. "So anyway, I think she gave me crabs."

My manager tells me I need to be on the other side to prepare for my entrance. Paul's award is given right after a brief intro by host Brooke

Shields. I remember how confused I was when I was about eleven years old and saw my first Playboy. All the men wore tuxedos. I didn't even know where one would go to get a tuxedo. It was a very confusing time for me.

I can't see when I walk onto the stage from the bright lights shining down. Luckily the teleprompter is only a few feet away and I'm able to get through my introduction of Paul without any real hassle. I'm not wearing a turtleneck and I do not feel like a liar, but I am still wearing my oversized aviators, so who knows what I'm saying. While Paul begins giving his speech, I duck backstage and almost run over Sandy, who takes a step back and just shakes his head. "Mickey, if you change your mind, you can always come over to my side. Look at you." There's an uncomfortable minute or so before he steps toward me and hugs me, slowly patting my back. "Simply marvelous." My manager calls me and tells me that there's an after-party being hosted by the lead editor of DAILY DISH, the local daily fashion paper, and that I have to be there and make sure I schmooze the editor.

I look back at the stage and see Paul exiting to great applause. Uma Thurman and John Travolta head to the stage, passing Paul as he comes off. Backstage, Sandy and Paul are face to face. "Congratulations, Paul, and nice work on Oprah. She's your only real chance."

"Sure, Sandy. Congratulations to you, too, and I hear you've been talking with Ralph?"

"Oh, you know, I talk to everyone in the industry. It's incestuous is what it is."

Both look out onto the stage, where Thurman and Travolta are recreating the dance scene from Pulp Fiction as their way to introduce Sandy. Sandy looks over at me and then back to Paul. "Oh, don't worry, your introduction was fine." Sandy laughs as he leaves Paul and walks onto the stage to cheers.

A model named Barry, I think, approaches to show me his latest tattoo. He has this thing where he gets ink of every place he's been. His last trip was to Dallas so he rips off his shirt to show me his tattoo of Texas, located just above Cancun, below Montreal. He is riding the new tattoo high and does not want to wear a shirt but does want to do a shot so we each have a shot of Patron Silver off the stomach of a girl named Lacey who giggles when my tongue touches her skin.

My phone rings and it's my brother, known as Cheeks. He did a spread for Playgirl a few months back and was just named "Ass of the Year."

Cheeks is not my biological brother but rather my adopted black brother. I was twelve when I met Cheeks. He was just starting a modeling career (as was I) and we quickly became friends because we were much better looking than everyone else and also because we both could tell the difference between good and shit weed. This was very important.

"Playgirl is flying me to New York for another shoot. I'll be there in a day or so, Mick."

"Rock and roll, dude. And congrats on the ass thing. That's cool."

My manager lets me know that there is a "P-cubed" party. I find Juanita and let her know. She's cool with it, even though she's not into the pill scene. "No problem, I brought some Train Wreck with me."

I take three Vicodin and grab all of the pills that look like Vicodin to add to my stash. I grab a vodka drink, light a Camel, and take Juanita out to a deck of either an apartment or add-on to a restaurant. It's hard to say exactly what is going on inside because of all the smoke. A guy wearing a cowboy hat and girl not wearing a shirt, only a bra, come out to the terrace and begin making out. Looking around, I realize I'm the only one out there, so I head inside. Closing the door, I hear the girl yell out and ask if I'd like to join them. I keep heading inside and look for Juanita. Dizzy, I grab a seat on a couch and close my eyes for a second. When I open them back up, a clown is sitting to my right. Just sitting there, staring straight ahead, drinking a Meister Bräu beer. I shake my head and look to my left, where another clown has sat next to me. With his large hands, he gives my hair a tussle, grabs my hand, and places it on his nose, then squeezes, leaving out a honk.

I run out of the room and Juanita stops me.

"Mickey, what is wrong with you?"

"The clowns!" I tell her. "The fucking clowns!"

Juanita looks around, then turns back at me, confused. "Mickey, there are no clowns."

I look, but it's blurry.

"Mickey, where is your shirt?"

I look down and see I'm not wearing a shirt. I look back at Juanita. "Why are you wearing a sombrero?"

Juanita spends the next minute staring at me and then grabs my hand. "What sombrero?"

My fourth sombrero story.

On our way out of the party, I think I see Jerry Seinfeld, but according to Juanita, it's only Nicholas Cage.

20

At a rooftop restaurant named Charlie's in midtown, Sandy and Ralph are having lunch. Sandy has a plate of oysters while Ralph is eating a blackened chicken panini.

A full mouth of chicken, Ralph says, "Let's say I'm over there, on that building." Ralph points at another rooftop across the street. "And for the sake of this discussion, let's say there's two guys standing in the middle of the road, down there." Ralph points to the road, then waves his hands around in the air. "And we're all on radio, you know, connected, and you get the call to take a shot at the guy on the right. Which one is your guy?"

Sandy puts down an oyster. "What do you mean? Which one of the two would I shoot?"

"Right."

"That one." Sandy points to the imaginary guy standing closest to them on the street.

Ralph jumps out of his chair and points to the street. "Exactly! You're right." Ralph sits down and waves as if to say the conversation is over. "I had to fire a guy last night. He insisted that the right side was the guy's right, not his right."

Sandy moves his plate of oysters off to the side. "I'm hearing things." He takes a drink from a chocolate martini.

Ralph grunts and takes a drink from his pint of Stella. "What, the Oprah thing?"

"Yes, the fucking Oprah thing, Ralphy. Do you know how much power she has?"

"I wouldn't worry about it."

The nonchalant response turns Sandy red, and he reaches across the table and grabs Ralph by the neck. "Listen to me. I can't lose to that prick ass Paul Johnson, do you understand? And I'm paying you damn good money to make sure of this." Ralph tries to loosen his grip, but to little success. Instead, he leans into Ralph, inches from his ear. "I'll fuck you until you love me, then we'll see who is the gay one at the table." Sandy releases his grip and leans back into his chair.

"Oprah brings in the middle states." Sandy licks his fingers then looks back outside. "Any chance we could..." Ralph stands up, "No, that's not an option, let's just stick with plan A."

"What is plan A?" Sandy backs up. "You know what, it doesn't matter. Do whatever it takes."

"I've got an idea. Where is Kung Fu Master today?" Ralph finishes his Stella.

"He's at Bloomie's, introducing my new perfume, Master."

"Perfect." Ralph is fidgeting for his keys, maybe looking for a cigarette. "Just perfect."

Sandy leans back in. "Why?"

Ralph laughs. "It's all part of plan A. That's really all you need to know, Sandy. That's all you really want to know. My work is like a Tarantino

71

movie. A fucking head rush. I'll call you when it's done."

21

I'm in the shower noticing how the acoustics at the Four Seasons are really great. When I come out there is a maid cleaning and I mention the bathroom acoustics. She agrees and says they are the second best she has ever experienced. When I ask her where the acoustics were better, she tells me that jail cells in Texas have even better acoustics.

Hearing this makes me curious and I consider my options with the maid, but then I pop a Vicodin and pass out on the bed.

When I wake my manager tells me I need to be on a plane to LAX. I arrive at LAX, where a limo meets me and takes me to Venice Beach, where I shoot a magazine advertisement surrounded by screaming fourteen-year-old girls for a body spray named RIPPED. I eat tacos near Muscle Beach and then from L.A. I hop on a puddle jumper to SFO, where the only redeeming characteristic of the airport is that it's not in Oakland. From San Francisco it's back to O'Hare for a connection that makes me feel like I've walked through half of Chicago. After the journey my manager calls me to tell me my flight has been canceled and the only way I can get back to New York is through Detroit. I call Juanita and ask her what she would do if she was me.

"If I was you, Mickey, the first thing I'd do is get an AIDS test." We laugh and decide Detroit is the best (and only) real option other than staying in Chicago, which isn't a realistic option when you think about how useless the city really is. The only worse-laid-out airport than Chicago is Detroit, I tell my manager as I walk miles to get to my connection.

In Detroit I notice a lot people stressed out, stressed out from missed connections, delayed flights, and just overall stressed from being away from home. Not necessarily being away from their families, but just the idea of being away from their "safe place," always protecting what they have, no open arms. Negative about the past, complaining about the future. This is their present, not seeing the world as plentiful, with an attitude that there is always tomorrow if things don't go perfect today. I look around at the ones without open arms and feel sorry for them.

Around midnight I arrive back in New York. I am picked up by a town car sent by Paul Johnson that takes me to a bus where several Designers and Executives are dressed in costume and holding various bottles of liquor. Paul hands me a bottle of pills and we get on the bus. Paul is the first to light up a joint and then everyone joins in. It isn't clear what is being celebrated, but everyone is happy and occasionally we stop to go into a deli or a liquor store to get more alcohol.

The next morning I fly to Miami for interviews and spreads with Women's Wear, GQ, Esquire, and

TAIL, which is an adult movie industry rag doing a "where are they now" article on me. My manager tells me I need to go to Boston.

In the airport at Miami I'm booking my ticket to Logan when I meet an ex-model named France who quit the business to join the porn industry like I did. "Fucking Europeans. Couldn't get any more work." I give him some contacts and tell him to go; letting him know I'm now working for Paul Johnson wouldn't help the situation. Plus, he'll find out soon enough when he walks by the newsstands.

At Logan International my manager fucked up my limo reservation and the taxi line is a mile long so I'm forced to take a train into the city. A man drinking a Coca-Cola closes his eyes for a minute; a homeless man approaches and grabs his soda. While the train moves he drinks down the beverage, only stopping near the end to offer the person he stole it from a sip. Terrified, the man passes, gets up, and moves to the back of the train, where he watches the homeless man, worried what he is going to do next.

A guy wearing a green Boston Red Sox hat sits next to me. He looks over his shoulder (the international sign for he's about to say something racist) looks over at the homeless man and then at me and says, "It's not the homeless that are the problem, it's the fucking—" He stops when the homeless man throws the soda against the side of the train. The man in the hat gets up and joins the others at the back of the train.

The truth is the homeless are not the ones to be terrified of; after all, these are the people who struggle with life and can't handle it. Believe me, this person will be the last person to commit to a fight. Maybe it's different here in Boston. In New York, I'm not scared of the homeless. The guys to be terrified of are the Wall Street guys ten million in debt and coked up—those are the real savages on the street.

In Boston I do a photo shoot on Newbury Street for a boutique named TELL ALL and then I have my limo take me on the Mass Pike, where I pop a Vicodin and check out the largest billboard in the city, a picture of me shirtless with the name Paul Johnson underneath. After passing by the sign, I take another Vicodin and wash it down with a bottle of Ketel One. The next morning I wake up and don't remember where I am. I hear someone yelling racial slurs in the hallway and then I remember. My manager tells me I need to be in Arizona and I tell him to fuck off, because there is never a reason to go to Phoenix.

22

DJ Powder is spinning records on the second floor of Bloomingdales. In between Shakira and 50 Cent songs DJ Powder meets clients in the bathroom, where he deals cocaine and sometimes heroine, depending on the season.

Strippers dressed as cheerleaders and men dressed as strippers dance to the music. In the center is a giant sign surrounded by balloons that reads: MASTER by Sandy Johnson. Kung Fu Master stands in the center. Flash bulbs all around. A smile on Kung Fu's face.

Kung Fu Master makes the rounds to the media, introducing himself and showing his signature karate chop, which Sandy told him is going to be his trademark. Overall he is very cordial and everyone wants to be near him as he moves from table to table as if each stop is an official appearance. No one is feeling the moment more than Kung Fu Master, who is laughing and doing high fives with the associates. During a song by Jay Z, all of the strippers circle him and dance extremely close. One of them, named Boise, takes off her top and buries his head into her chest.

After fifteen minutes a few members of the media begin asking Kung Fu Master questions on the upcoming show, but before he can answer, seven men wearing hockey masks and dressed in camouflage storm the department store and grab him by the hands and legs, carrying him out while he screams for help.

Kung Fu Master has been kidnapped.

Five minutes later, a press release is issued. Paul Johnson is suspected to be responsible.

23

Sandy steps out of his meeting and answers his phone.

"It's done," is all he hears.

24

"This one is the Kawasaki 600E, a favorite of Canadian lumberjacks," says a man wearing a stained Yankees baseball cap as he lays the chainsaw on the conference table. "Now this one," the man reaches into a box next to the table, "this is the Sears 300 Turbo. It's a little classic, but still gets the job done." He looks around. "What are you looking to do?"

Paul looks at the two chainsaws laid on the conference room table. "I'm not interested in classic—especially Sears, the shredded wheat of tools. What is this, the Roaring Twenties?" Paul looks around the table. "That's a joke. It's okay to laugh."

The man grabs the last one from the box, a Cleveland Tools saw known as the Terminator. "Now this one is especially loud. This is the one they use in those movies, you know, Texas-Chainsaw-Massacre-type movies."

Paul picks up the Terminator and holds it in the air. He sets it down and then slowly moves his hand up and down the chainsaw. His index finger runs along the chain. He laughs and then asks if he can hear it. The man in the stained hat grabs the Terminator and pulls the cord, releasing one of the most horrifying sounds ever heard throughout the office. Two sewers actually slip and cut themselves, many run for the exits, and Gayle, from Finance, hits the fire alarm.

Paul holds it up, waves it around his head and smiles, and then shuts it off. "I'll take three."

25

Spread out on the table in front of me is my current supply of pills. I'm back in New York. Juanita and I are staying at The Four Seasons for a couple more nights. I count 39 Vicodins, 35 various "speed" pills, and approximately 50 Ecstasy pills.

Ever since the pill party, I've decided I may not be able to handle three Vicodins at once. I had this experience once with cocaine, where I snorted ten grams of cocaine in two hours. I don't remember anything from that night, but the next day my girlfriend at the time told me I was found completely nude on a raft on a lake two towns away. After checking my bank account, I realized I had spent over thirty thousand dollars on the ten grams. That's when I knew it was time to slow down. It wasn't the money, just the fact that I'd allowed myself to get ripped off.

Not getting ripped off when buying street drugs is the twenty-seventh secret to being famous.

Two weeks later I went to a party in New York and woke up the next day in London. After this I had my first stint in rehab.

Juanita is completely nude, sitting on a chair with her head bent back as she dyes her hair purple. Her feet are resting in a small tub of water. I go to the floor and do 1000 sit-ups then go back to the desk, where I put the Vicodins in a bottle and throw the rest of the pills into the hotel waste basket.

My manager tells me I have a meeting in Tribeca with Paul around 6pm. I look at the Bose alarm clock stereo next to the bed and it's only 4pm so Juanita and I smoke a joint, watch an episode of The Simpsons, and the next thing I know I'm woken up by my manager letting me know that my limo is waiting for me.

26

I meet Paul in the lobby of THE PLACE 2B, a brothel fronting as a luxury condominium building. We sit on leather couches in a lobby-type area with a private bar and private waitress service among other things. The walls are all mirrors, as is the ceiling, as is the floor. Women are walking in lingerie and I can cut a line anywhere in the building. Maybe I never woke up from the pill party?

Outside the door I hear a man pounding, trying to get in. A man wearing what appears to be a bulletproof vest appears out of nowhere, grabs a baseball-bat-sized baton, and lets himself out the door, sliding through only a small-enough opening to let himself out. The door seals, tightly, creating a suction-type sound when it closes. Still, we can hear the cracks of the baton. After five minutes the man wearing the vest returns, walks over to us, and apologizes for the commotion.

A waitress approaches and Paul orders a bottle of champagne, a brand I've never heard of, and then asks me, "What do you want, Mickey?" followed by a muffled laugh.

Our champagne arrives in minutes. I try to get a glance of the label on the bottle, but the waitress, who is only wearing a black teddy, puts the bottle in a bucket of ice quickly. Paul takes a drink and smiles. "Mickey, I'm not sure if you heard, but

Sandy's number one, some Kung Fu Fucker or something, was kidnapped. Pure publicity. Bullshit the way he's trying to put this on me, but here's the thing..." Paul puts his glass out to cheers; we knock glasses. "I've got some ideas surrounding Oprah, so I'm going to use you first, showing off the line of self destruction, then for the finale I'm bringing out Oprah."

I take a drink of the champagne. "Cool with me. Big plans for Oprah?"

Paul laughs. "Headline plans, Mickey, headline plans." Paul laughs again. "Remember, this show isn't about the best line, it's about the most publicity. Whoever wins that battle wins the war." The waitress comes back and whispers something to Paul. After she leaves, Paul tells me our rooms will be ready in ten minutes. "It's cool, Mick." Paul points up and around. "It's Jewish. They know how to take care of their customers."

I just nod, not sure what that has to do with anything and also not sure what in the hell I'm doing here.

"I can't have my number one entertainer have any stress." The waitress comes over and fills up our glasses. "This place will take away the stress and then some." Paul leans back into his chair. "There's one girl here, she's all bottom and wears panties with a print of the American flag. I call her the Liberty Bell."

Paul stares at me as I picture Paul and the Liberty Bell.

"But don't worry, Mick, that's what I like. For you, I got something special." As soon as Paul finishes this sentence, the waitress comes over and lets us know our rooms are ready.

My room is empty when I open the door. About three thousand square feet of space complete with two Jacuzzis, a stocked bar, and a fridge full of champagne. On top of the bar is a bowl of cocaine. I walk over to the bowl, considering, when I hear a knock at the door. Three girls are at the door, one blonde, one brunette, and one Asian. All dressed in lingerie. Once the door is cracked they push it open and then push me back to the bed.

"We are Snap, Crackle, and Pop, and we're here to take care of you tonight, Mickey. Tonight you take the night off, and we're going to take off our clothes."

Snap adjusts the lights. They begin flickering, and the three girls strut around the bed as if it's a runway. From the walls, house music begins playing, deep beats and loud sirens. One by one, the girls, they climb onto the bed. Snap undresses, throwing her clothes over her shoulders, and then rubs me. Crackle jumps up and bends over, allowing me entry from the rear, and then Pop slithers up and then pounces on top of me, treating my body as a trampoline as she dumps champagne all over me. As the champagne hits, the music changes to a heavy rock guitar. I look over and see a man with long hair in the corner of my room, jamming on the guitar. Snap and Crackle are licking off the champagne, purring as they do this.

The whole ordeal takes between fifteen minutes and five hours. Time is impossible to keep track of. After the girls are done, the guitarist jumps up on a television stand and does a three-minute solo, throws his guitar pick at me, and says, "Rock on, my man."

On my way out I see a disheveled Paul Johnson in the lobby. He's holding an almost-empty bottle of champagne and is missing a shoe. "Now that, Mickey, that's self destruction."

27

A phone bounces off the wall. "Mother fucking cocksucker! I'll kill him! I'll fucking kill him!" Paul screams. He has just gotten word that the AP has picked up the kidnapping with speculation that Paul is behind it.

Paul grabs his cell phone and calls a childhood friend named Joey, who calls his brother Anthony, who sends a guy by the name of Bobby over to Paul's office.

Standing in his office, smoking heavily from a cigar, Paul walks behind his desk, where his knife set is, and grabs a short butcher-style knife, then he calls in a person named Tani, whom he's never met from Marketing, and fires her.

28

"You have got to be shitting me! Fuck this, I won't let him win." Sandy slams both fists down on his keyboard. Sandy has just gotten word from his private investigator that Paul has a contract with Oprah and has purchased chainsaws. "Oh, the lack of humanity in that. Oh, that fucking savage!" Sandy calls Ralph and has him come over to his office immediately. Years ago, when the Johnsons were on speaking terms and not the giants of the industry quite yet, they often went out for martinis and discussed their ideas. C + C Music Factory was usually playing when they had these discussions. Sandy specifically remembered one idea where Paul talked about having male models wielding chainsaws and chopping up a female model. Seeming odd to Sandy, he asked, "So it's going to be like a horror movie? You're going to film it? Like a fake snuff movie?" Paul just laughed at Sandy. "Fake snuff movie? No way, I'd do it for real, on the runway."

29

My manager sets me up an interview with the Associated Press to discuss the exhibition. For the most part they are basic questions related to the line of self destruction, whether I have any information on Kung Fu Master, and what I've been doing the past few years. For the most part I deflect all of my questions and just focus on how excited I am to be showcasing Paul's work. For a second I swear I see Snap, Crackle, and Pop holding CBS microphones, but it was only the lighting. New York Magazine asks if I'd heard the latest comment from Tyra on models, and since I haven't, I reply with, "I'd do her." The audience eats it up. Secret number sixteen on how to be famous: don't talk to Tyra. Thirty minutes into the press conference, my manager notifies everyone that we are finished. I flex one more time to cheers from the media and then we're off.

30

"I wouldn't say I see the good—I don't. In fact, I hate most things, but the fact is, it's just not that big a deal to me." I grab a Camel, but again Dr. Shames waves no, saying I can't smoke in his office. "I always believe I can do whatever I want."

Dr. Shames actually gets out of his chair and removes the unlit Camel from my hands. "So what you said earlier, about those who protect their own, you think it's not right, that they are wrong?"

"I wouldn't say wrong, but what a shitty way to leave. You need to live for the moment. Don't you agree?"

"To an extent," Dr. Shames says, a phrase that pretty much says he doesn't agree or disagree, a typical doctor's response. Dr. Shames continues, "You see, Mickey, not everyone can live in the present. Not everyone is like you. You, Mickey, have the power to change."

"What do you mean?"

"Well, I can see it. If you want to change something, take control, you have that power."

"I guess."

"Wasn't it you who just told me to live for the present and know that another adventure awaits tomorrow?"

"Something like that."

My second therapist, Dr. Wendy Mandrino, was a lesbian shrink who also, like Dr. J., was great at reducing stress in my life, keeping me clean and focused on my career. The fact that she was a lesbian also made it much easier to concentrate. Of course, during our third session I think there was some chemistry detected and for a second I could have had her. Of course she wanted a shot at Mickey. What girl wouldn't?

After several sessions, already caught up with the back story and beginning to analyze my current issue (I was considering changing my shade of blond and switching from oversized to regular sized aviators), Dr. Wendy thought it would be a good idea to tell me a little bit about her back story and how she got to where she was. This is where it all changed.

Apparently the advice started in the non-conventional way. Unable to get a job out of school, Wendy took up her second love, cooking fried food. Always creative in marketing her ideas, Wendy began taking orders on Craigslist. Yes, that Craigslist. The one where you find apartments and hookers into feet fucking. Once Wendy's customers learned of her trained background, they began asking questions that she would answer and discuss. "I created my initial client base from Craigslist!" With excitement Dr. Wendy shouted this to me. Those were the last words exchanged between us.

31

Bobby shows up in a pinstriped suit and very shiny shoes. He's a full foot taller than Paul, and that's without the giant cigar Bobby's smoking.

They chat for a few minutes; Paul shows Bobby a couple pictures and explains the situation.

Bobby says something about a girl and Paul yells at him, "This is the most important job of your life!"

Bobby lifts his cigar and asks Paul if he heard about the private investigator who was found in Brooklyn.

"The one with the needles stuck in his head? That fucking guy looked like Hellraiser."

"Yeah, that's the one." Another drag. "That was her job. Some dealer stiffed one of our clients, and let me tell you, she didn't even get paid that much." Bobby sets down his cigar. "Trust me, she's good. Real good."

Back looking at the pictures, the words "cocksucker" and "faggot" and "slime" are heard over and over. They then walk to a locked office where there is a safe and Paul makes a very large withdrawal.

32

My manager tells me I need to be at the gym, where I use the Stairmaster for thirty minutes, run on the treadmill for thirty minutes, and then work out with a medicine ball for another thirty. Then my manager tells me I need to meet a producer who is interested in casting me in a movie for a drink.

A life of checkpoints. Go here, then there, meet him, eat here, shake his hand, the limo will be waiting, sit over there, walk here, take the plane to, smile.

Exhausted when I get back to The Four Seasons, I'm greeted by a naked Juanita and a freshly prepared T-bone steak from room service.

When is enough enough? After my porno movie *Big Bang IV*, I no longer had to work. A series is key in the business.

The first *Big Bang*, I was the third listed in the credits, then in *Big Bang II* had moved up to the feature male, and followed with *Big Bang III* and *IV*, making the series a franchise. After *BB IV* I was a modern day celebrity, even winning six awards at the adult movie awards in Las Vegas. I was unstoppable, but I knew I had to come back. Back to the place where the insanity has escalated to unparalleled heights, where my boss is planning some type of takeover of the media.

Maybe it's the attention, but doesn't that change? Doesn't everyone have to change? Does anyone have the power to change what's around them, let alone themselves?

Juanita guides me to the middle of the floor, where she unbuckles my pants and slides her hand in. With her other hand she takes the T-bone platter and places it on her head. She tells me to eat the steak.

When is enough enough?

As I take a bite of the steak, I look down and see Juanita's bobbing head, blowing me. I wonder if maybe I'm the one person who doesn't have to change. It's an interesting thought that stays with me until Juanita makes me cum, which is ironically when I'm on my last bite of steak.

33

Paul calls me at 8am to tell me that "Every second spent learning is a second not spent thinking." Unable to get back to sleep, I sit on the couch, watching The Flintstones, smoking a joint. I come up with an idea for a Flintstones episode where Wilma and Betty take a trip somewhere, leaving the boys behind to babysit Pebbles and Bamm-Bamm. Fred decides to run a daycare center. Fred runs the door (cash only), Barney is in charge of children's games, comedy ensues.

I go to grab my pills, but forgot where I put them. I search the bathroom and then the bed, under the pillows and mattress. I'm about to begin cursing out Juanita when I remember I have a bottle stashed inside a sock deep in a drawer because I was paranoid someone was going to steal them.

After an hour, I call back Paul and tell him I want to continue to stay at The Four Seasons through the end of the show. He laughs and tells me that now I'm starting to think like him. I order an egg sandwich from room service. While waiting for it to be delivered, I read *Where*, then I eat the sandwich, take one of my Vicodin, and go back to bed.

34

"So it sounds like you enjoyed yourself last night." Today Dr. Shames is wearing a brown blazer, tan slacks, and no socks.

"Yeah, Juanita is great. Not sure what I'd do without her." I look over at the window, consider walking over to it, but don't have the energy. "Plus the steak was cooked perfectly." I stay on the couch. "I just don't want to fuck things up."

"But you're scared of not having affection, having people love you," Dr. Shames leans back, "people needing you."

"No, I think—no, you may be right. I want to change. I do believe. I'm just not sure I have that kind of discipline."

"Control."

"No, discipline."

"No, control. You need to control the situation. That is how you feel safe. You know how we were discussing how some people are afraid to take chances because it's not safe? Well, for you, not having control is not having that safety we all need."

I shake my head, not sure how much of this I can take.

"You need attention to feel safe, but you want to change. You can control this, Mickey, but it has to be on your terms."

A moment of clarity. "I need to sacrifice myself for the greater good?"

Dr. Shames nods approvingly, then shakes his head sideways.

"I didn't say that," says Dr. Shames, but I don't hear him. I'm already out the door.

My third therapist only lasted two sessions, but this one was not terminated by me or the judicial system, but rather by her. Paula Cornerstone had been asked by one of her neighbors to dog-sit for them while they went out of town. The second day they were gone, the dog died. A full-size German Shepherd, dead on the floor. Unable to get in touch with her neighbors, she was told of a pet cemetery in Queens, right off the subway. Paula stuffed the dog in a large duffel bag and began dragging the dog to the subway. When she approached the stairs, she struggled, dragging the bag down the steps. A man in a cardigan sweater assisted, carrying the back of the bag down the stairs and into the train. When asked by the dapper dressed man what was in the bag, Paula replied, "Just stereo equipment."

Five stops later, the train arrived at Paula's stop. The pet cemetery stop. As Paula got off the train, the sweater man offered to assist, helping with the bag off the train and then up the stairs onto the street. At the time it didn't seem strange that he had gotten off on the same stop. He was wearing a cardigan sweater so it was clear he wasn't completely sane. Once they reached the top of the stairs, the man turned to Paula and punched her in the nose, sending her tumbling down the stairs. With blood pouring down her face the man lifted the bag and ran down the street. After the incident, Paula moved to West Virginia and took up gardening.

35

"**B**ut you're a woman. Are you sure this is going to work?" Paul repeats over and over to Libby, who is sitting in front of him. She is the person Bobby has sent over to take care of Paul's problem.

"Oh my God! You do know I can have any guy eating out of my hand, right?" Libby crosses her legs seductively. "Let me see that cigar."

She reaches for Paul's cigar, but he pulls it away. "You do know he might be gay, right?"

"Oh, those are the easiest, honey. You just got to let me do what I do well." Libby stands up and moves toward Paul. Libby shrugs. "You heard about the Hellraiser guy, right? I know Bobby likes to tell that story. You see, each job has its own solution. This isn't a cookie cutter business."

Paul nods. "Yes, I heard."

"What the fuck, you want a resume?" Libby moves up, in front of his desk, leaning over. "Trust me, the Hellraiser guy? He got off easy compared to most."

Libby moves close enough so that her thigh is brushing up against Paul's thigh. She reaches over him, letting one of her breasts touch his cheek, and grabs one of his knives out of the case. She puts her knee in his crotch and the knife against his throat.

Paul throws the cigar at Libby. "Get the fuck out of here and go do your job!"

36

"So, what are you, some boy terrorist or something?" Sandy asks the Middle-Eastern-looking man who is sitting across his desk.

"No, sir, I am Shareef, and I am very American."

"Fuck me, not sure if it even matters." Sandy dramatically throws up his arms. "Well, Ralph says you're the best. We'll see. Oh, fuck me."

Sandy leans in close, moving both hands evenly across the table, until both rest on Shareef's knees. Sandy squeezes, releases, and then squeezes again. A wink with his left eye, then another wink, followed by another squeeze of the knees, and finally another wink.

Sandy pulls back his arms. "Move along now. Good luck."

37

Cheeks dumps out a mound of coke on the table. "Oh, shit, is this cool?"

"No problem, it's cool," I tell Cheeks.

"Thank God. I'm used to my L.A. clubs, wasn't sure about the big NYC."

Cheeks and I are in the lounge area of the new club LOCO. There are live gorillas in cages in the far corner—presumably high, by the way they are moving back and forth—and hanging from the ceiling are cages containing extras. Actual extras from television shows and movies, just nondescript people standing inside the cages. They are not paid, only hoping to get noticed.

Cheeks goes to the bathroom and I can hear the mirrors being taken off the wall for lines. It is very rare to walk into a restroom after Cheeks has been inside and be able to get high off the residue on the mirrors. He actually carries tools with him to assist with removing the mirrors—too many broken mirrors already in his past, no need for any more.

Back in the club, looking down at his shoes, Cheeks bends down and wipes a speck off his black what appear to be Italian made shoes. "I never like the shoes I have on." He looks over at my feet. "See, like right now, when I bought these, money was no object; I just wanted the most badass shoes I could find." Cheeks look down at the table of cocaine, then looks back at my feet. "Now, I look at your shoes and those look like the coolest mother fucking shoes I've ever seen." Cheeks points up to a cage where an extra who is wearing Nike cross-trainers is staring down. "And look at those—fucking cool."

Cheeks does a line and then the waitress comes by, notices me, and shakes her head while looking at Cheeks. "It's a good thing you're with this guy." She points over at me and giggles. I order a flight of Spanish champagne. Cheeks orders a scotch and water then looks over at me. "Dude, did you just order Spanish champagne?"

"It's cool, bro. Spain is the new France."

"Cool," says Cheeks. "Hey man, I think I may have a little problem with the..." Cheeks looks down at the table, "the powder."

"Oh man, why do you think that?"

"Cause man, I've probably spent 35K in like six months on blow."

"Oh shit, dude. You really need to... Uh, wait a minute. Did you say 35K in six months?"

"Yeah."

"Oh, that's not a problem. 35K in six hours, that's a habit."

I lean down and do a line. "Let me tell you a story about a friend I know—well, used to know. I mean, I guess I still know him, but... Anyway, my friend Tate decided to get into the entertainment industry, sort of, as a magician."

"Oh no, c'mon, man, this isn't going to turn into a clown story, is it?" asks Cheeks, then I contemplate telling him my three-Vicodin-night story, but pass. "No clowns. Now listen.

"So he makes it as a magician. Eventually he's got a ton of gigs, has his own magic mystery type store. He's fucking made it, man."

Cheeks does another line. "Then what?"

"He starts doing coke and goes bankrupt, all gone. Everything."

"Damn."

I do another line. "Now that's a man who had a problem.

"True."

I cough, then add, "You know, the ironic thing was that in the end it looks like he had one more trick left in him."

"Oh yeah, what was that?"

"He made an entire business disappear in one month."

I lean forward. "So if you do need help, let me know. I know guys. It will be painful, but I do know the right guys.

In between songs, DJ Bomb, who is wearing a knit hat despite the temperature approaching ninety degrees, takes a minute to give a shout out to me, introducing me as the pimp of the fashion world. I give him a wave and then he dedicates his next mix, titled "Pimpin," to me.

A person wearing clown makeup is standing in the corner, sipping a Heineken. I shiver and Cheeks catches me.

"You okay, bro?" He looks over and sees the clown. "Oh, you got a clown thing?"

I give a nervous laugh. "Only when they're doing normal things, like cashing a check, using an ATM," I look over, "or sipping a damn Heineken. That just ain't right, man."

A black woman walks by Cheeks slowly, showing off her backside, then turns and smiles.

"Man, I love those girls. It's that Liberty Bell look, you know?" I nod as if I've heard this phrase before, then Cheeks says as he continues to watch her walk away. "Oh shit, the Liberty Bell, it's the new hourglass."

Cheeks grabs one of my glasses of champagne. "To the ass of the year!" I cheers Cheeks, and he responds with, "To the model of the year, congratulations, Mickey!" We clank glasses and drink down the champagne and then my manager tells me we have a potentially serious problem.

38

My manager tells me that his private investigator has information that I'm being watched and he worries that I may be kidnapped in response to what has happened with Kung Fu Master. A bodyguard is being sent over immediately. My manager tells me that the only instruction is not to be farther than five feet from him at any time and that he will be armed. My manager also tells me that this is just a precautionary measure.

Paul calls and tells me, "A temporary state of perfection is as close as we can get, and when we reach this, well, let's just say anything can happen."

I tell him what my manager said and this infuriates Paul, launching him into a tirade where he swears Sandy Johnson is behind it and when the show is over he'll never design again.

"Let me ask you something, Mickey. If you could be a genius and never have sex or have sex all the time and be an idiot, which would you pick?" Paul sounds as if he's eating something.

"I guess not having that much sex couldn't be that bad, so I'm saying the genius one."

Paul is definitely eating something, maybe an apple. "No, you don't understand. No sex at all. You aren't allowed. So it could be torturous if you're a genius, because girls love passion."

"Man, I'll think I'll take a rain check on this one. What's your pick?"

I hear something dropped, maybe an apple core into a wastebasket. "Have to go for the dope that gets the sex. You know, even Einstein, you just know he was showing his sketches to chicks."

Tiredly I tell Paul, "I'll take a rain check."

39

Later in the day, Sandy Johnson holds a press conference to announce that Kung Fu Master is back. His captives drugged him and kept him blindfolded and beat him for several days. He remembers very little but through a statement has said he was fed a non-stop diet of cold pizza and warm RC Cola. He mentions that the media has blamed Paul Johnson and he pauses. Sandy's way of not disagreeing with this statement.

The press release is read in front of a group of reporters and extras hired by Sandy. When he says the words "drugged", "Paul Johnson", and "RC Cola", there are gasps in the audience.

Because of this, Sandy will not be giving access to Kung Fu Master until the day of the show. He will also not be pressing charges because they are behind schedule, and "despite these tragic circumstances, the show must go on." When the media asks about speculation of who is responsible, Sandy's only response is, "I think it's quite obvious who has the most to lose with my number one model out of the picture. I mean, c'mon, warm cola? The man is a savage, people!"

40

Juanita and I have breakfast at DINE in the Upper East Side. Mason, my bodyguard, eats with us and then watches us have Bloody Marys at Boathouse, where several fans recognize me and approach me for autographs. As each one approaches, Mason does a quick pat down to ensure my safety.

A dysfunctional band that consists of a lead singer with a cowboy hat, an electric guitar player with his eyelids pierced, and steel drum player are playing "New York, New York" over and over. The steel drum player is nicknamed Salmon because he has a couple of groupies calling out to him.

Our waiter approaches and I order a second Bloody Mary, handing him my empty glass. It turns out that he is not our waiter but rather a reporter, who is embarrassed.

Juanita says something about no rush getting back to our room.

"Do you ever feel like everyone is rushing to get to their safe place, like home, or their hotel room?"

"Oh, definitely. Half of America is rushing home to do what, watch TV? They'll say it's to go home to the family, but how many families are there today? Not many. Oh shit, I dropped my straw." Juanita watches her straw fall to the floor. I call the reporter over to retrieve another straw.

Juanita and I agree the world is fucked and there is a need for change.

Next, my manager tells me to go to the gym, so Mason and I work out (he hits the weights, I use the elliptical machine). After the gym, my manager tells me about Kung Fu Master and that if I have a bodyguard it may be bad press, so I let him go. During lunch I receive a call from Cheeks, who informs me that he and a couple of new friends just got an eight ball and want to know if I'm interested. Exhausted, I pass, and Juanita and I go back to our room to rent a movie. We agree on nothing too violent and rent an Eddie Murphy movie. After the movie we split a joint, have sex, and then while Juanita is taking a shower there is a knock at the door.

41

Libby is noticeably uncomfortable when she is asked by Dr. Shames about her profession. "I won't go into details, but let's just say it's not a desk job."

"Okay, so let's start with why you're here. You mentioned stress from rushing—yes, that was the word. 'Rushing' is the word you used."

Relieved Dr. Shames didn't stay on the topic of work, Libby relaxes a little bit. "Yes, I feel like life is passing me by too fast. No time to, how do they say, stop and smell the roses."

"Interesting," is all Dr. Shames can say. Then he adds, "When do you feel safe?"

"Safe?" Libby looks lost. "I always feel safe. I can definitely take care of myself."

Dr. Shames shakes his head. "No, that's not what I meant. I mean, when do you feel safe, secure in your world?"

"Oh." Libby pauses. "That kind of safe? Yeah, I don't think I've ever felt safe."

42

Outside of Sandy Johnson's building, Libby watches the lobby. Mostly tall, slim men wearing skinny jeans and big watches exit the building. She watches the windows and hacks into the network, checking emails and next steps he may be planning to take.

She receives a call. It's from Paul, and he has confirmed action, signed on the dotted line. "Just fucking take care of it," he says and then hangs up the phone.

Libby had been in the industry for five years now, starting out on a small freelance project in Canada that had been set up by a man named Craig who had hair like Ronald McDonald and smelled like cheese. The man he wanted killed had raped his sister, not that the details are that important, but it does feel good to know when this is the case. Makes work almost enjoyable. When she goes to find Craig's hit she finds a man, ready to die, waiting for her. Libby does her job and leaves. It felt more like an assisted suicide than an actual hit.

After that, Libby worked with a major financial firm on Wall Street. This one firm kept her for three years until a disagreement with her supervisor cost Libby her job and forced her to permanently remove him from his position. Since then, Libby has been freelancing, working through vague ads on the internet and word of mouth. Only recently has she made contacts in the fashion industry, where work seemed to be plentiful.

43

There will be seven pieces on display for Paul Johnson during the show. Mickey will be wearing the two main men's pieces and Oprah will wear the final piece, a dress the color that Paul has described as blood. Paul is reviewing the items as several Technical Designers measure the garments on fit models. As Paul discusses the garments, everyone in the room takes notes. The Designers, Merchandisers, Production Associates. The Presidents. All take copious notes as Paul discusses the garments and how this "show" is going to change everything as they know it.

"FIRST!" Paul yells. "First we will send out a collective group of our usuals. These will be like our fluffer models, preparing the crowd for our treasure, Mickey. Once Mickey makes his two passes down the runway, then—and I hope you are all ready for this—then Oprah Winfrey herself will be walking down the runway with this..." Paul has his assistant bring in the blood-red dress. "This is what Oprah will be wearing when she walks down my runway.

"Team, get your resumes ready, because in a couple of days we are going to reach perfection, and when you reach that state, complacency is right around the corner." No one in the room understands what Paul is saying, but they all write down every word.

That night Paul invites Juanita, my bodyguard, and I to a small anniversary party on the Upper East Side. When we arrive it appears we are late because everyone has their champagne up and are toasting Paul and another woman. We quickly understand that this is just the first toast and that every ten minutes there will be another. When I ask Paul what everyone is celebrating he explains, "Ten years since my divorce." A divorce anniversary party. I think of this and then the words "wood chipper" and "erection" enter my mind so I go looking for the bar.

At the bar a woman is wearing a red dress and is holding a red drink that she catches me looking at. "It's cranberry." She winks, and then says, "Cranberry with crushed Ambien and a splash of vodka." I nod and wink back, she leans in, lightly bites my ear and whispers, "Ambien is the new Vicodin." I look back to the bartender, who is shirtless, and order a vodka rocks. He begins rubbing the ice cubes on his chest and I want to ask him about Manny, but Juanita shows up and says she wants a drink like that, pointing to the woman in the red dress drinking Ambien and cranberry.

I walk over to where Paul is talking to two hot blonde girls and an actor who may have starred in the Iron Man movie when he sees me coming and asks, "Hey Mickey, you ever have Five Guys?" I pause and then realize he is asking about the hamburger place, so I respond "No, just three guys and four blondes!" Which is actually true and this leads to two pats on the back, a spilt drink, and an ironic high five. Paul grabs me and pulls me to the side, "Mickey are you okay? You know everyone important should have one of those." Paul points over at the body guard. "Don't worry, just, you know, you may want to stay away from the ice."

After our heart-to-heart I find Juanita, have another vodka on the rocks, and ditch my bodyguard.

44

Shareef has been here before. Waiting. Waiting in his FedEx uniform. It's how he spends most of his time. Watching, and waiting. Watching people eat, walk in the park, work out in the gym. Waiting while watching a movie. Knowing the right time. The right time to walk into the five-star hotel, the right time to walk up to the room, the right time to knock on the door.

While waiting, thinking. Thinking about how surprising it is that more women don't commit crimes considering the prison factor isn't as bad, as in guys-on-guys type of action. Do women have a similar problem? Doesn't seem right. Shareef's concentration is lost when he brushes his hand against the bulge in his pocket. Last night, Shareef left with a couple hundred in twenties. Now he has a giant bankroll of five- and one-dollar bills. Was it the beers or strippers, and why did he pay for everything with a twenty-dollar bill? Thinking back, he remembers at the end of the night buying a pack of Dentyne from a vendor on the street. There is a very good chance he used a twenty-dollar bill to make this purchase. Shareef looks at the time.

The right time is now.

45

Sometime around noon, Kung Fu Master is moved from the J headquarters to the W hotel. Still unsure what happened to him, it really doesn't matter since he's back to his pampered life and is enjoying every minute. The bounce of the bed, the softness of the pillow, the artwork on the walls. He walks over to the window and stares out at Times Square, looking up and down the street he'd been on a thousand times. A thousand views, but not this one.

Kung Fu Master grabs a bottle of wine from the mini-bar and prepares a hot bath.

Born in Japan as Ernie Suzuko, he never knew his father. Around the age of 10, Ernie moved to New York, searching for the American dream, with his mother, who got a position as a nurse and for a while was able to support them before she fell to the drug of choice during the Eighties, crack cocaine. Living on the streets, Ernie fought for everything and tried his hardest to get his mother help before she was too far removed, eventually passing. Ernie was on and off the streets, fighting his own addictions to heroine, then meth, then booze, beating them all. A funny thing happened along the way—Ernie became a leader on the streets, a person who knew each nook and cranny, each corner and who was in charge. Ernie educated the homeless men on how to get off the streets, and taught the women self defense. This is where Ernie picked up the nickname Kung Fu Master on the streets. A local legend, not quite as famous as the Naked Cowboy, but more respected.

At no time had this become more apparent than the time he organized a march of over five thousand homeless people in front of City Hall in an attempt to stop the closing of five soup kitchens that have helped prolong lives already sentenced to doom.

Unfortunately he had never had a chance for love, nor had he ever had a chance to be with many women that wasn't drug payment related. He was a true local hero, with thousands who would listen when he spoke and act when he acted. He was even the spotlight of a local television special focusing on the homeless and their daily fight. It was during that program that Sandy saw the combination of charisma and social pity that made him realize Kung Fu Master would be perfect for his show.

After his bath, Kung Fu Master receives a call from the lobby that he has a message. Stopping off first for a tall beer at the hotel bar, Kung Fu Master grabs his message from the front desk. It reads: I GOT YOU A LITTLE SOMETHING FOR TONIGHT, ENJOY — SANDY. Kung Fu Master looks around but doesn't see anything so he goes back to the bar and has a couple more beers.

During his third beer, Kung Fu Master engages in a conversation with the bartender over the chances of a meteor that has recently been spotted hitting and destroying the Earth.

"I like its chances," says the bartender.

Kung Fu Master nods approvingly.

A girl wearing several pearl necklaces approaches Kung Fu Master and asks for his autograph. He obliges as she mentions how big of a fan she has become and can't wait to see him on the runway. Kung Fu Master gives her a kiss on the cheek and then tells her to remember that anything is possible, then he turns back to the bar and continues to drink his beer.

After his fifth beer he feels a tap on his back. It's a beautiful girl who says Sandy sent her.

"Do you want a drink?" Kung Fu Master offers.

The woman smiles and puts her hand on his thigh. "Why don't we go up to your room?"

Upstairs in Kung Fu's room, the woman tells him to get comfortable and that she will be right back as she ducks into the bathroom. Nervous and excited, Kung Fu Master goes to the mini bar and gets another bottle of wine, pouring some into two hotel glasses and placing them next to the bed. Unsure how to get comfortable, Kung Fu Master tries the lean on the side with shirt unbuttoned look, then on the stomach with his hands cradling his face. Neither look seems to be working for him. Then, realizing his foolishness, he grabs the remaining bottle of wine and drinks straight from it. He then leans back on the bed.

A toilet flushes, and Kung Fu Master doesn't know what to think about that, but the excitement is growing.

When the woman comes out, Kung Fu Master looks her up and down. Really no surprise here—in fact, he rather expected it. His last thought was how someone supposedly with so much street smarts never saw a professional hit coming.

It only took one shot, center of the head, and Kung Fu Master was dead.

She stares at Kung Fu Master for a moment, then walks over to the side of the bed, leans over, and gives him a kiss on the cheek, making sure she pulls her hair back to avoid getting blood on her. "Too bad—he was pretty cute for a homeless guy. Just really needed a chance," Libby says to no one, knowing this is going to be her last job. Not necessarily a decision that's pondered—the job lets you know when it's over.

Libby removes the silencer, places the gun back into her bag, and leaves the hotel through the front lobby.

46

I open the door, look down, and see the box the delivery person is holding. The box looks like it came from Vietnam or some Third World country. In the seams I see black dirt, possibly weeks old, being held by the person's left hand. He has very hairy knuckles and is having trouble clutching the box. His hand shakes. I turn to look up at the other hand.

The bullet rips into my stomach. I look up to see a man holding a gun, maybe a nine-millimeter, inches from my face. He pulls the trigger. Nothing. The gun jams. At the same time, Juanita comes out of the bathroom, screaming. I grab my phone to call 911, but my phone is ringing. It's Cheeks. I answer the phone. My brother can hear my pain through my scream as I bring my blood covered hand up from my stomach. I look back to Juanita, then look at the man frozen at the door, still pulling the malfunctioning trigger. For some reason I want to say she has nothing to do with this, but instead only scream "SHE!" into the phone. The man dressed as a FedEx delivery person runs out, Juanita is still screaming, and in the distance I hear sirens. This is the last thing I remember.

47

"**I**s he dead?" Ralph asks from the rooftop of a deli in Brooklyn as he stares into the city.

Shareef fumbles for his words. "He might be. I'm not sure." Pause. "He was losing a lot of blood."

There is a noise behind them. They both quickly turn to find two rats playfully running around an air conditioning unit.

"And she saw you?" Ralph asks.

"Well, she was in the shower."

Slowly, Ralph walks around Shareef, once, twice. Shareef turns his head, watching Ralph look at him and then back over to the island. Finally stopping, looking up in the sky, he says, "Why me?" He cries, "Oh, Sandy isn't going to like this," then pulls out a gun that was stuck between his shirt and the back of his jeans. He slowly puts the gun to Shareef's head.

"Did she fucking see you?"

"Yes."

With the gun still on Shareef, he reaches into his pocket and pulls out a small notebook and pen and throws them down onto the roof. "Draw me a map."

Shareef nods. "Okay, but I don't think they're at the Four Seasons anymore."

Ralph slaps Shareef with his gun, dropping him to his knees. "The hospital! Draw me a fucking map! Just write down the fucking address!"

Shareef opens up the notebook and writes down the address and then draws a couple of lines showing where the hospital is. He grabs the notebook and pen and stands back up, handing both to Ralph.

Ralph looks at what Shareef has written. "Well, okay then. We need to take care of this." Ralph motions for Shareef to start walking toward the fire escape. Shareef breathes deep when he sees that Ralph is leading the way. Then Ralph turns around and shoots him in the head.

48

At the hospital, Juanita is standing in the waiting area, crying and staring at the pastel green wall. A nurse walks by. "Pastel green is the new yellow."

The pastel green is the same as the pink green in the mental hospitals, the same yellow pastel in the retirement homes. Death is a lot like Easter—lots of pastels.

A woman wearing a blood splattered yellow dress is coming through, medics on each side, to the emergency room. Two kids follow, screaming. After the kids, a Scottish brute looking guy comes in waving a clipboard, yelling something about having the wrong health insurance for the hospital.

Next to Juanita sits an older woman, almost asleep. A boy wearing a blue bandana and Converse shoes, who may or may not be part of a gang, sits quietly next to her.

Over the speakers, R.E.M.'s "Shiny Happy People" is playing softly. Elevator music has turned into hospital emergency room music.

Over the check-in counter, a bulb is burning out. The light flickers while the receptionist wipes blood from the counter left from the last patient. The receptionist takes a sip of a Red Bull and coffee concoction she drinks to get through a shift.

Cheeks barrels through the waiting area doors, incredibly high from all of the cocaine and screaming obscenities as he staggers forward.

The far corner, there is a crazy person wearing a Stevie Wonder wig playing a small keyboard. In between R.E.M. songs you hear the man singing "Messin' Around."

"You crazy bitch, how could you do this!" Cheeks pulls out a gun and shoots it toward Juanita, hitting her in the shoulder. Then before she can scream anything else, he shoots her in the head. Blood splatters through the waiting room. Panic. Juanita falls to the floor, where a pool of blood forms around her head. Cheeks pulls out a bag of coke, dumps some on his hand, and snorts it.

R.E.M.'s "Losing My Religion" begins playing.

The crazy person wearing the Stevie Wonder wig approaches Juanita's body, noticing a tattoo on her lower back. He jumps back and proclaims, "At least the woman died with ink!"

During the commotion, a middle-aged man attempts to grab the elderly woman's purse and run off with it, but the boy wearing the bandana tackles him, causing both to slide into Cheeks, knocking him over, sending his gun flying across the floor. Regaining his composure, Cheeks gets back on his feet.

Cheeks looks over at the counter. The receptionist is hiding behind her desk. The light continues to flicker. On the opposite side there is a clock, but he is unable to tell the time because it is covered in blood. He looks at the boy who has recovered the purse. The boy is looking over Cheeks's shoulder, so he turns around.

The receptionist pops her head up for a moment and she reminds Cheeks of the wife of a lawyer who helped him beat a marijuana charge a few years back. He notices her fake tits and figures he probably paid for them. Cheeks turns.

Standing there is Ralph. He locks eyes with Cheeks and then shoots him in the head. Cheeks immediately drops to the floor next to Juanita, blood emptying from his skull. Before the two pools of blood meet each other on the floor, Ralph runs out of the hospital. Behind him, orderlies and interns follow, but at a cautious distance. Blood pours behind.

For those remaining, R.E.M.'s "End of The World" begins playing.

49

My manager tells me fame has its price. He tells me fashion is a state of mind. My manager tells me I have the power to change things. The same manager who has called me a god is now saying maybe I need to step back and see things for what they are. My manager tells me I have the power to change the way things are. I need to step out of my comfort zone. It's for the greater good, I'm assured. He tells me these things even though I'm in a state the doctors are referring to as a "light" coma. I dream of hosting a yard sale, out in the country—though this is not your average rummage material, but rather pills. I am running a yard sale for pills. A stack of money sits in front of me. Most of the pills have been sold when a man in a dark hat approaches and asks how much for my bottle of Vicodin. This is when I begin to shake.

My manager can hear R.E.M. playing somewhere in the background, off in the distance.

50

The media has put the body count at somewhere between four and fourteen, depending who is reporting. It is known that the homeless man known as Kung Fu Master is dead. Sandy has asked the city put their flags half mast in honor of Kung Fu Master. Mickey is lying in a deep coma at a location now unknown because there was an assassination attempt after his arrival to the hospital, leaving both his girlfriend and brother dead.

Oprah has rescinded her offer to appear in the show. She is appalled that it has yet to be cancelled. Neither Paul nor Sandy Johnson is making himself available for comment. Both will address the media during the show tomorrow that both now insist must go on.

This just in: The New York Times is reporting five dead, dozens injured, and the police suspect foul play related to the upcoming showdown. The Daily News is reporting six, possibly seven, dead, and the lead they have received is that a fashion serial killer may be responsible. The serial killer is rumored to be tall, dark, and maybe anorexic. The New York Post has run a special edition with the cover RUNWAY GUNDOWN. Seventeen now reported dead in connection with The Johnsons. Terrorism is suspected.

51

Libby meets Paul in the middle of Sheep's Meadow, a large open grass area in Central Park. It's dusk and the park is closing down, but Libby needs her payment before she leaves town. The NYPD is in full force, applying heat to a city in the spotlight, and Libby is an important piece to the puzzle. Also, after leaving her last job, she felt pain, the way the job lets you know it's time to move on.

She sees Paul, wearing a long coat, standing in the middle of the park.

As she approaches, she notices he's holding a bag, which he extends. "Good work, Libby. You were right—you can do your job and do it well." He pauses and brushes his hand toward the West. "Walked past one of those German pubs, the ones where they're all holding giant beers." He shakes his head. "Why can't they just get two beers? Why do they need glasses that large?"

"Thanks." Libby grabs the bag and opens it, counting the money.

Paul stands as Libby counts the money. "So the report said he was found half naked."

Libby looks up. "Yeah."

"Well, it's a little strange, don't you think?"

"Not a big deal, but you do know you're about five grand short, right?" Libby pauses for a second. "What exactly are you insinuating?"

"Let me put it to you this way..." Paul coughs then continues. "Do you know who the most dangerous people are?" Before Libby can respond, Paul continues. "They're the guys wearing two different colored shoes, or screaming obscenities. You know—the guys who just don't give a shit."

Libby shifts her weight. "I don't know what you're trying to say to me, Paul."

Paul laughs. "Five grand, yeah. Well, there's a lot more than five grand I can give..." Paul grabs Libby's hand and pulls her until their thighs touch.

Libby tries to pull away. "I..."

Before she can say another word, Paul sticks a knife into her lower back then pulls up, slicing her open.

On her way down, she is able to pull out her gun and get a shot off, which grazes Paul's leg but creates a loud noise. Paul kicks the gun out of her hand and shoots her in the head, grabs the bag of money, and begins running when he hears someone yelling behind him.

Paul runs past Wollman Rink, past the Chess and Checkers house, stopping for a second to catch his breath and listen. Someone is still following. He continues to run, cutting in between Delacorte Theater and the new Great Lawn, finally ending up by a pool somewhere near North Meadow that he didn't know existed in Central Park.

In front, four black men are approaching him, someone is gaining from behind, and he can hear sirens in the distance.

Paul puts his hands up when the black men approach.

"I've got forty thousand dollars here and I'll give you a hundred thousand more if you can get me out of here." Paul breathes heavily. "Someone is following me."

52

"So what happened to your guy Shareef?" Sandy asks Ralph as they ride up Madison Avenue in the back of Sandy's town car.

Ralph cracks the window. "There were problems, Sandy, and I was forced to micro-manage."

The car is spotless but smells of old food, maybe rotten fish. After inhaling deeply, Ralph makes a face and looks back at Sandy, who just shrugs, unsure what the problem is.

"And Mickey?"

"Last I heard, he was in a pretty deep coma." Ralph pulls out a cigarette and lights it. "As you probably have already heard, there were witnesses."

Sandy nods at Ralph. "I heard." He looks closer at Ralph. "What are you smoking?"

"Marlboro Lights."

"Oh." Sandy leans forward and tells his driver to pull over. "Looks good, but I'm a Parliament man myself." Sandy cracks the tinted window to allow some air to come out. "I've always smoked them. It's strange—even when I drink, I always have the same drink, a Tom Collins. Never felt the need to switch." Sandy rolls the window back up. "I guess I'm loyal, like a dog on all fours."

Sandy looks out the tinted windows to see where they are. "So I've got a pile of bodies and the one job I wanted you to take care of, well, isn't taken care of."

"It's not your problem, Sandy, trust me, and Mickey, believe me, nothing is coming of that."

Ralph lowers his window even more, blowing smoke out of the open crack. Sandy's driver continues to look back whenever Ralph uses the window controls. Ralph begins fidgeting with a lock control and then an intercom that beeps in the front each time it is pushed in.

As Sandy gets out, he looks back at Ralph. "Let's hope for both our sakes that he doesn't pull out of his coma."

Ralph takes a big drag. "I hear that."

Sandy's driver rolls down the divider. "Cool enough for you?"

The Grateful Dead is playing in the front. Ralph is moving the window up and down. At first he allows the window to close and then fully open and then he goes half-way up and then back down. The driver stares at him.

"What do you think about the *Wake of the Flood* album?" Ralph asks.

The driver shrugs his shoulders. "Not sure. Never heard it."

"That's surprising. Most people who listen to The Dead have all of their albums. What about Phish, do you like their music?"

"No, they're the Goo Goo Dolls of drug rock. No, I don't like Phish." The driver turns back around and grins at Ralph. "You cool enough?"

"Yeah," says Ralph. "Just right."

"Good." Sandy's driver turns around and shoots Ralph between the eyes. "Glad you're comfortable."

He then rolls up the window. "I hate it when fucking people touch my controls."

53

My manager tells me that to accomplish the greater good I have to do my job. I hear Dr. Shames's words telling me I have the power, the gift to change. My manager tells me everything is set up for me to succeed, not necessarily change everything, but change the overall direction. My manager says this is about me, but also others. My manager tells me everything will be fine, trust him. The show must go on. This is the last thing he says before I wake up in the hospital bed.

My doctor is standing over me. I have a pain in my stomach. "Hold still," he continues to say. I try to get sentences out, but nothing is coming. The doctor explains to me that I was shot, and I remember part of it, at least the painful part of it. He tells me I was very lucky, no major organs, only blood loss. I flinch, and he informs me the physical pain should go away soon.

I ask the doctor for Vicodin and he willingly gives me three to take.

Despite not being able to concentrate well, I know something is up because the doctor said the phrase "physical pain" and was way too willing to hand over the Vicodin.

I pop the pills.

The doctor informs me of Juanita and Cheeks.

After hearing this, I ask the doctor to leave. I wait for a few minutes for the Vicodin to take effect.

After about ten minutes, there is little pain and luckily no clowns.

My fourth therapist, well, I never actually got his name. That's not entirely true. I got his name but was never introduced. The day of our first session, I seated myself on the couch and was about to light a Camel when the cops busted in and arrested him for dealing OxyContin. Later, I would read that for each prescription written, two were picked up. Good gig while it lasts. After all, we all need our pills, right?

Paul Johnson enters the room carrying an issue of *GQ* with Bono on the cover. I'm crying. Paul hands me a tissue and puts his hand on my shoulder.

"Did you? How in the fuck?" A tear falls down my cheek.

Paul steps back from my bed and looks down on me.

"Are my hands covered in blood? Is that what you're asking, Mickey?"

I nod.

"No. Sandy murdered Juanita and Cheeks. I know this, and yes, there are others. Let me put it this way."

Paul pulls out a cigar, then looks around, realizing he's in a hospital, and puts it back. "Earlier this week, the media, those fucking scoundrels, they asked how I thought I would do in the show tomorrow. I told them I guarantee success." Paul clears his throat. "Now, let's be honest, a lot of that was for show, but let me tell you this." Paul leans in. "Truth is, when there is only one contestant, you can guarantee victory." Paul stands up, walks to the front of my bed. "Mickey, there's a little known law in New York. You can't be charged for a crime if you're checked into a psychiatric ward at the time of being arrested.

"You see, Mickey, temporary perfection is a state of mind. Tomorrow, you'll be a part of history." Paul takes a deep breath. "Don't worry, get a good night's sleep. Tomorrow, history will be made. You will understand more—everyone will.

"The day the fashion industry self-destructs."

The feeling of being terrorized passes after I take two more Vicodin.

"See you tomorrow, Mickey."

54

Words are chosen carefully by Paul and Sandy on the morning of the show. At the Mayor's request, the NYPD has agreed to hold off questioning until after the show, given the amount of money to be generated and the fact that neither Johnson is directly indicted for any of the deaths. At this point any murder in the tri-state area is being treated as potentially linked to Seventh Avenue. The New York Post is now estimating sixteen bodies could be linked to the Fashion Show Conspiracy. What is not clear is who is behind it, since both of the Johnsons have been hurt. The Post is calling it an all-out "Runway War!"

In the front row, right side, sits Burt Reynolds next to Michael Jordan next to Hillary Clinton. Cannons over the top of the runway are shooting confetti into the crowds. In the back, the last round of cocktails are being served fast as guests hurry back to their seats. Angelina Jolie is sitting next to Jenna Jameson, who is sitting next to Alec Baldwin.

Paul Johnson walks out onto the stage. Everyone jumps to their feet. Paul Johnson raises both of his hands. Confetti shoots out over the top of the front rows into the middle, where Jon Stewart sits next to Jessica Alba, who sits next to the Olsen twins.

The music is a potpourri of destruction. The start of Guns N' Roses' "Welcome to the Jungle" leads into Metallica's "Battery," which leads into the Sex Pistols' "Anarchy in the U.K." Backstage, a new model named Riki has just puked his guts out on Lamar's feet, creating shoe crises, leading to tears.

Past the models and clothing is a table full of chainsaws. A technician named Alan is oiling them, ensuring a smooth startup.

Mickey is standing by himself. A girl named Toto comes up from behind him and grabs his left cheek. Mickey doesn't even acknowledge this move, eyes focused on the runway.

The music stops. Paul motions for everyone to sit down. "Ladies and gentlemen, my line of self-destruction, the new black."

55

Backstage, I'm trying not to pay attention to the pain in my stomach. The pain reminds me of a childhood trip through Iowa. The cornfields on each side made me feel like we were in a car wash the whole time and I got carsick. That's how my stomach feels now, stuck in a corn car wash I can't get out of.

Luckily I'm wearing a kick ass iced out scorpion chain to distract from my not-so-perfect abs today. Just to be safe, I drop to the floor and do another hundred crunches. Flash bulbs pop as the first round of models, the "fluffers," walk out onto the runway. I will be next. I feel a hand on my shoulder and turn. It's Paul.

My fifth therapist went crazy. Dr. Isaban Kumall decided to embrace minimalism to the point of no return. Initially, he sold his new house and moved into a small apartment, leaving his family behind. Next, Isaban was living out of only ten boxes, then five boxes, then three boxes, until eventually he left his apartment. With only an ATM card, Isaban wandered the streets, living in his office. When the bank was unable to reach him, they froze his account and Isaban went from a minimalist without a home to just homeless.

Around the curtain Paul asks if I see a woman wearing a yellow hat. I do. "That girl, she was my first true love." Paul pauses, then says, "Did you see the sky this morning? There's no way we're going to jail today." Before I can say anything, he's back on the girl wearing the yellow hat.

"We were young. It was a mess, but she has never missed one of my shows."

"That's cool," I say, watching the models make their turn and make their way back.

"They always win, Mick," says Paul. "The women always win in the end." He pauses then adds, "Sometimes you think it's not that way, but you're just fooling yourself. It's like a rookie who goes surfing, catching that perfect wave, and for a second all is good until, finally..." Paul lets it hang. It's my turn to go.

"Wipeout," is what I hear as I hit the runway.

56

Paul Johnson's line of "Self Destruction" starts off well with approving nods from the audience. There is buzz that Oprah is in the building and will walk the runway despite the body count, which according to the NY Post continues to rise by the hour as bodies turn up throughout the city.

I walk out. Flash bulbs are popping, and there's a noticeable flinch as I walk. Walking down the runway I see George Clooney sitting next to Megan Fox who is sitting next to Dr. Phil. As I make the turn, I look over at Julia Roberts and blow a kiss. More flash bulbs. Definitely not my best walk, but given the circumstances, I receive a standing ovation.

There is a pause and then Oprah walks out wearing the blood red dress. The crowd rises to their feet as Oprah struts. Behind her are three men wearing suits designed by Paul Johnson. The three men are carrying chainsaws, which they fire up. Oprah appears unfazed, but everyone is standing in horror as the men begin twirling the chainsaws in the air, inches from Oprah.

Backstage, the crew runs to the side to watch. In fact, everyone is focused on the stage. Backstage, Sandy is standing alone. Not wanting to give more attention, he stays back, saying a silent prayer for Oprah.

"It's just a diversion," says Paul.

Paul is standing behind Sandy. "It's not really Oprah and the chainsaws. Well, I'm not going to use them on the lookalike, but the fact is, everyone in the world is focused on the stage. You see, I'm not the savage you think I am, but I will do whatever it takes to win."

"Touché," says Sandy.

Paul pulls out his gun and puts it up to Sandy's temple.

"I am order. You are disorder."

With the chainsaws going full blast, the gasp of the crowd, and the screaming of the Oprah lookalike when one of the chainsaws nicks her arm, no one hears the gun go off. No one hears Sandy's last cry for help. No one hears him drop to the floor. Paul watches him fall and stares, the blood leaking from his nose, ears, and mouth. It didn't have to be this way, it just was.

Bob Saget runs into Tom Brady who runs into a Hilton who runs into an Olsen twin. Two TMZ camera men try to balance as everyone stampedes toward the exit. The scene—the scene is murderous.

Paul walks out onto the stage. He stops where there are drops of blood and takes a bow. Camera crews are three blocks deep. Helicopters are hovering over the top.

Ladies and gentlemen, we now interrupt your regular scheduled programming to bring you this breaking news. Sandy Johnson has been murdered.

That feeling when passengers on a train have been notified that their conductor is unconscious, it probably feels similar to this.

Paul Johnson has officially taken over the media.

www.ingramcontent.com/pod-product-compliance
Lightning Source LLC
Chambersburg PA
CBHW030612130626
46552CB00002B/522

ABOUT THE AUTHOR

David S. Grant is the author of several books including *Corporate Porn* (Silverthought Press), *Bleach|Blackout* (Offense Mechanisms), *The Last Breakfast* (Brown Paper Publishing), and *Hollywood Ending* (SynergEbooks). David lives and works in New York City. For more information, go to http://www.davidsgrant.com.

then turns back to his soup and wonders if he needs a new pair of slacks.

My manager tells me it's time to leave. I take my last Vicodin, walk out, and hail a cab. Paul's lifeless body falls to the floor, where a pool of blood is collecting.

"Take me to Saint Joseph's Psychiatric Ward at 91st and Lexington."

The driver turns around and asks, "Hey, aren't you that guy from the billboard?"

"Which one?"

THE END

"It's not noon yet. I can't eat a sandwich, that's why I tried," Paul points down to his plate, "this. I also can't have breakfast for lunch or dinner, just isn't right."

I order a chicken sandwich.

This is a good time to mention that Paul is out on bail with a "pending investigation" that is running parallel with a "pending insanity plea."

"You see, that's where you're wrong," says Paul. "I'm the one who creates. I'm the one who destroys and then builds."

My manager tells me this is bullshit.

"Bullshit. It has nothing to do with the clothes. It's just me. I'm the one. I'm the Savior in the eyes of the consumer. I wear the clothes and look the way they want to look."

Paul leans in. "You got some fucking... Mick, let's talk this over now. We can build whatever we want."

I lean even closer. "I guess it's like you said, I got to thinking."

My manager tells me to grab my gun from my pants.

"It's just me, Paul. It has nothing to do with you. In fact..."

My manager tells me it's time.

I pull the gun up and point it at Paul. "The world is better without The Johnsons."

My manager tells me to kill Paul Johnson.

Across the street a man wearing a red sweater is eating his chicken soup when he hears a gunshot. He slowly lifts his head and turns to the sound,

57
One month later

My manager tells me I need to meet Paul for breakfast. I've had a long morning session with Dr. Shames. The type of meeting where I did most of the talking. At the end we—well, I—decided we need to take some time off, and when we reconvene, I want a clean slate. I want to start from the beginning.

Paul is sitting by himself at a table near the window when I meet him. In front of him is a half-eaten plate of eggs. "I don't recommend them." He points to his plate, then stands and gives me a half-hug, faking a sucker punch to my stomach.

I sit down and pop a Vicodin. One left.

"I told you, temporary perfection. I had them. I'm the savior." Paul says.

I smile and order a coffee. "Doesn't matter. I'm the one everyone wants to be."

Our waitress approaches. She is anorexic. I can tell from the caved in face and perfect teeth. Had she been bulimic, well, the teeth are the giveaway. Which is better, it's hard to say, but she is wearing the hell out of that Marc Jacobs low-cut dress. Anorexia versus bulimia: To never have loved, or to have love and lost?

I look at the menu and debate whether to have an omelet or a sandwich. "What do you think?"